HUNTER'S CHRISTMAS AND OTHER STORIES

VAL PENNY

First Published by in 2023 by SpellBound Books

To my friends, Chris and Len, with love

PRAISE FOR VAL PENNY

More gripping stories about DI Hunter Wilson, DS Jane Renwick and others by Val Penny. The author weaves stories of family, power, politics and revenge to enthral her readers.

Erin Kelly, bestselling author of Broadchurch

Stories with a thoroughly engaging cast of characters, developing and growing through expert writing. This is a collection of thrilling and engrossing stories.

Michael Jecks, bestselling author of the Templar series

These stories form another great addition to the DI Wilson Crime Thrillers series. A must read for crime fiction fans.

Retired DCI, Stuart Gibbons, bestselling author of Being a Detective

Hunter is a terrific character, always a pleasure to read about and here he leads a cast of old and new acquaintances. A great read - thoroughly recommended.

Simon Hall, bestselling author of the TV Detective series.

INTRODUCTION

THIS BOOK CONTAINS THE FOLLOWING SHORT STORIES

Hunter's Christmas
The Bruntsfield Book Group
Cruel and Unusual Punishment
In Plain Sight
Cats and Dogs
Heads You're Dead
Visit to Venice
The Party
The Corpse in the Catacombs
My Father's Garden
The Fall
The Second Chance

HUNTER'S CHRISTMAS

HUNTER AND MEERA CAME OUT OF THE TRAVEL AGENT'S ARM IN arm. A car drew up beside them and three men dressed in red and a skinny one in green got out.

"Gosh, who knew there were three Santas?" Meera smiled. "But look, they're parked on a double yellow line. What are you going to do about it Detective?" She asked Hunter with a grin.

"Nothing. It's Christmas. I'm not going be guilt-tripped by locking up Santa, let alone three of them!" He smiled at her and took her arm. "I'm so looking forward to our holiday, nothing is going to spoil it. Imagine, we'll be spending Christmas in India. I'm also glad to have a decent length of time off."

"Yes, and it'll be lovely for us to be together with my family. They all want to get to know you better. We should practice your Hindi before we leave."

"Good idea. And at least it will be warmer than it is here."

Meera smiled. "It's not just the temperature here in winter, it's the wet and the wind and the icy pavements."

"I know all about your views on Scottish weather my darling, but if I stay to discuss that now, I'll be late for my darts match, and you know how angry that makes Jim and all the team."

"Of course, you go. I'm going home to finish packing. We haven't got long before we go."

Hunter kissed Meera gently on the cheek and jogged along to the car. He was looking forward to this match. It was the last one of the season and would take his team to the top of their league if they won.

He stopped at an ATM in Princes Street to get some cash. He took a moment to observe the Christmas market in full swing and the tree covered in white lights on the mound. Edinburgh is such a beautiful city, he thought.

Hunter turned his attention back to the ATM. He decided it would be a nice gesture to get a pint for each member of the team. They usually had a Christmas Eve friendly, but he wouldn't be able to make that this year because of the holiday. Somebody else would be drafted in to take his place, he knew that.

As he put his money in his wallet and turned away from the ATM he found himself facing the same three men dressed as Santa Claus as he had witnessed parking earlier. They were arguing and cursing about an elf who had stolen their tips, which of them got paid the most and who should buy the drinks, while they waited to use the cash machine.

"Look, lads," Hunter said, "I saw you parking on a double yellow a few minutes ago. That's bad enough, but Santa certainly shouldn't be cursing and swearing this close to Christmas. What if a kiddie hears you?" Hunter asked.

"What business is it of yours? We lost all our tips to a thieving little elf!" shouted the tallest Santa. "I'll kill him when I get my hands on the thieving little snot."

"And like we care about the fuckin' stupid kiddies!" The smallest Santa exclaimed.

"The only folk worse are the bloody awful parents." The fattest Santa grumbled. "And the job's only good for six weeks then it's back on the brew."

Hunter found them really exasperating. "Aye, enough," he said sharply. "Look, it's Christmas. Let me solve the argument and buy you boys a pint, you do a good job." He pulled his wallet out of his pocket and retrieved a twenty from the bundle.

The biggest Santa looked at Hunter's money and smiled. "That's a nice wadda cash."

Then it all happened fast. The smallest one snatched Hunter's wallet, the biggest Santa pushed him, and the fattest Santa knocked him over. Hunter slipped on the icy pavement and went down with a thud. He heard his wrist break as it hit the ground and his leg snapped. He howled in agony.

The smallest man saw Hunter's ID fall out of his wallet. "Fuck! He's a bloody copper!" He grabbed the cash and then quickly threw Hunter's leather wallet to the ground.

"Run!" the tallest one shouted.

The three Santas fled as fast as they could, scattering in different directions, leaving Hunter painfully rolling on the ground reaching to get to his phone with his good arm. He called an ambulance before he passed out.

As the paramedics carried Hunter into the Royal Infirmary of Edinburgh's Accident and Emergency ward, Ailsa Myerscough hurried towards the patient.

"That's DI Hunter Wilson!" she said. "Hunter, Hunter what happened?"

"You know this man?" the paramedic asked.

"Yes, Parijat, I know him well. He's my brother's boss. What's happened?"

"The cop brother?"

"I've only got one."

"Well, his boss here was jumped at an ATM at the West End of Princes Street. There's a poor young copper standing there now to preserve the scene, but this guy's got a compound fracture of the left femur and a broken left wrist. He's had morphine for the pain and fluids to stabilise his blood pressure. He was out cold when we found him but drifted in and out of consciousness since we got him into the ambulance."

"Who did this, Hunter?" Ailsa asked.

He smiled at her. "Santa Claus," he said.

"Yeh, okay. Take him to cubicle five. We'll need two units of blood right away, Joan," Ailsa spoke to the senior trauma nurse. "You get that hooked up. I'll call his fiancée and my brother and then we'll work out if we can operate on that leg or wrist tonight, or if it'll need to wait until tomorrow."

"I doubt we can work on both the wrist and the leg together," Joan said.

Ailsa nodded. She walked towards the exit of the hospital and pulled out her phone. She called Meera who said she would be at the hospital within half an hour. When she phoned Tim and told him the news there was a short period of silence. She heard him telling his friends Bear and Mel what had happened.

"Did the boss tell you who did this?"

"Santa Claus," Ailsa said.

"Santa Claus, huh. Was he concussed?"

"Probably."

"Look, I'm at Mel and Bear's flat and we've been drinking. I'll have to get Kenneth to drive us over. See you asap sis."

"You could get a cab." Ailsa wasn't sure the trip to the hospital merited disturbing their chauffeur, Kenneth. However, she knew Tim would want to be by his boss's side as quickly as he could and at this time of year, with office parties and clubs full of revellers, calling Kenneth from his slumbers was doubtless quicker than waiting for a taxi or even an uber.

Hunter was already being prepped for surgery to get his leg straightened and pinned before Tim arrived at the hospital with

Bear and Mel. Tim saw Meera sitting in the waiting room drinking coffee from a machine. She looked sick.

"It's a bad break. Ailsa arranged for the consultant to lead the surgical team tonight. She said it'll give Hunter the best chance of a full recovery." Meera looked up at Tim. "He was only going to get some cash for a few drinks with the darts team. I left him to finish our packing. If only I'd been with him, it might not have happened."

"None of this is your fault, Meera." Mel said as she sat beside the other woman.

"It's certainly not. But we'll find whoever did it. Don't worry about that." Bear growled.

"Just don't let the boss see you drinking that muck," Tim said. "You know how he feels about decent coffee." He sat down on the other side of her and took her hand. "What happened?"

"I have no idea. We'd been to the travel agent to pick up our tickets and finalise our flight check-in. Then I left him to go to his darts match while I went home to sort out the last few things I needed to do."

Ailsa walked over. "Meera, they said you were here. I've just finished the surgery on Hunter's leg. It's a bad break." She sat opposite Meera and looked straight at her. There was no point in trying to minimise the injury, Meera was a medical doctor herself and the senior pathologist in the region. "Let's go somewhere more private so we can discuss it."

"I'll get us coffees from the machine, if you promise not to tell the boss." Mel smiled.

Meera stood up. "You can all come with me. That way you can tell the DCI and save me having to get upset and making a fool of myself," she said. "Hold on, that's a call coming in from Jim. It'll be about the darts match and why Hunter's late again." Meera stared at her phone.

"Let me speak to Jim and then I'll come and join you." Tim took the mobile from Meera and spoke softly to give the darts captain the news. The men agreed that Hunter would have to be discounted from the team for the next couple of months or until both his leg and wrist were fully recovered, then Tim stepped quietly into the family room to listen to his sister's summation of the injuries.

"It was a bad compound fracture of his left femur, and his left wrist is also broken. I suspect he put his arm out to try to stop himself from slipping on the ice and his wrist hit the ground first. His leg was twisted and that will have caused the break to be as bad as it is. He'll be with us for a while."

"Oh no." Meera looked at Tim. "We're meant to be with my family in India over Christmas."

"That's not happening. Not for Hunter, anyway," Ailsa said.

"And Tim told us the boss said Santa attacked him. Poor guy must have hit the ground with some force, and got concussed," Bear said.

"The paramedics said he was near an ATM at the West End of Princes Street, there may be some CCTV we can look at and that might show the attack." Mel suggested. She scowled. "This coffee is really rank."

"When can I see Hunter?" Meera asked.

"He's in the recovery room right now. You stay here and I'll come and get you when he's awake but do remember he'll be groggy from the anaesthetic."

"She knows. She is a doctor, sis."

"I could do with something to eat. Shall I go and see if I can find us a bite?"

"Bear, you're always hungry, but yes, see what you can find." Mel sounded exasperated.

"It'll just be junk from the machines this late. Do you want me to see if I can find a sandwich for you?"

"Yes, please Ailsa. I'll try and find crisps to go with it."

"Not for me, I couldn't eat a thing." Meera looked up at Bear. "I feel so helpless. I wish there was something I could do for him."

Tim reached out and held Meera's hand. "I know. It's miserable any time but especially when you had such a wonderful trip planned.

Hold onto the fact that he'll be fine, it'll just take a while for him to get back to himself."

"He'll be furious he's missed his darts match too," Bear said. He walked back into the room with several bags of crisps and emptied bars of chocolate out of his pockets. "This is all I could find."

Ailsa popped her head around the door. "One round of tuna and two egg salad. That's all that's left. She laid them on the table.

"Does anybody like egg salad sandwiches?" Mel asked.

"Me." Bear grabbed a packet and tore it open.

"To be fair, you'll eat anything."

"Not butternut squash. I don't like that. Or broccoli. Or aubergine. But these are okay." He waved an egg sandwich in the air,

Silence fell over the group. Meera stared at the door, Tim gazed at his shoes, Mel played a game of solitaire on her phone and Bear polished off the sandwiches. Time seemed to pass slowly until Ailsa came back.

"He's awake. He's asking for you Meera. Don't expect him to talk any sense, but he's awake. I'll take you to him."

Meera smiled. "At last."

"Meera, do you need us to wait and give you a lift home?" Tim asked. "Otherwise we'll get off. I want to be at work early to speak to the DCI and get the investigation started.

"You've not left poor Kenneth to wait for you, have you?" Ailsa asked.

"He insisted."

"No. I've got my car, Tim. Thank you. I'll be okay once I've seen him and spoken to him."

"Then we'll get away. Send the boss our best. I'll pop in tomorrow."

"He's where?" DCI Allan Mackay asked.

"Royal Infirmary, sir. He slipped on the ice yesterday evening and has broken his leg and his wrist." Tim explained.

"He must have bumped his head, too. He said Santa did it." Bear added.

"He's meant to be on holiday with Meera, India isn't it?"

"Yes boss. But he won't be going anywhere for a while."

"Bloody hell. I'll cancel his leave. You two get over and find out from him what went on. Let me know."

"Could we get fingerprints from his wallet?" Bear asked.

"Unlikely if it's leather. And Santa wears gloves!"

"True, maybe Colin and Nadia could look through the CCTV from around the cash machine? It might give us something to go on, sir."

"Yes Tim, good idea. They're observant. If there's anything, they'll see it."

There was a knock at the door. Desk sergeant Charlies Middleton stuck his head around the door.

"Sorry to disturb your pow-wow, but my lads have been called to Castle Terrace car park. They found the body of an elf on the first floor. Missing his hat and his head bashed in."

"And a merry Christmas to you too Charlie." Mackay muttered. "We have more important things than your attempts at humour to deal with. DI Wilson was mugged last night and is seriously injured in hospital."

"Really? Who did that?"

"Santa," said Bear and Tim together.

"Well at least he's still alive. My elf is dead. Nasty head wound apparently. My boys are keeping the site clear, but I think you should get some of your folk and CSI over there pronto."

"What? You mean this isn't a joke?"

"Well, a dead elf is sort of funny, except it's not when it looks like murder."

"Fucking shit!" Mackay slammed his fist on the desk. "Right, I'm going over to speak to Hunter. Tim, we'll take your car."

"Yes, sir."

"Bear, you get hold of the CSIs and find out what they've found out about Hunter's mugging. Then get them over to Charlie's elf."

"Yes sir." Bear couldn't help laughing.

Mackay lifted his phone. "DS Reid? Ah yes, Colin, I want you and DC Chan to contact the Royal Bank of Scotland and The City of Edinburgh Council. You need to examine the CCTV around the West End ATM and the Castle Terrace Car Park. DC Zewedu will fill you in. And can you get DCs Grant and McKenzie to come to my office."

"Yes sir."

Mackay nodded to dismiss Bear and began to gather his things to allow for a swift departure with Tim.

"What have I done now? Mel whispered to Bear as she and Angus McKenzie passed him in the corridor outside Mackay's office.

"Nothing. An elf is dead."

Mel sniggered and was still grinning when she and Angus walked in.

"What's so funny, DC Grant?"

"Something Bear said, sir."

"Well I need you both to Castle Terrace car park. It looks like a Christmas elf has been attacked and died."

"That's terrible. I thought Bear was joking."

"And take PCs Neil Larkin and Scott Clark with you. You'll need to relieve the poor sod who's been guarding the site, and you might need them for door-to-doors."

"In a car park, sir?" Angus sounded incredulous.

"Shut up and get out! Myerscough, you're with me."

"Yes, sir."

Hunter was awake when Mackay walked into his ward, just ahead of Tim. Meera was sitting by his bed.

"You well, Hunter?" Mackay barked.

"I've been better, sir."

Tim winked at Meera. "I stopped off at the shops, boss. Brought you some grapes. That's what they told me you give people in hospital. I got you this skating magazine to improve your glide for next time too."

"If that's meant to be funny young Myerscough, you've got to work on it."

"And the team clubbed together for this chocolate Santa."

"Tell them all, next time they want time off, they're fucked."

Tim grinned. "I'll do that, boss. Seriously, how are you?"

"Sore. Bloody sore and this leg is damned uncomfortable. Grab a seat both of you, and I'll tell you what I remember. Meera, love, you don't need to hear all this again. Could you get us all a decent coffee from the *Costa* downstairs?"

Hunter watched her leave and settled down to explain all he could remember to his colleagues. Mackay asked the questions while Tim took notes.

"Ooh, Mr Wilson." One of the nurses stood at the end of his bed. "Who are your visitors?" She stared exclusively at Tim.

"Two of my colleagues, Jessie."

"Well if you're not going to introduce me, you can't be needing any more pain relief."

"Staff nurse Jessica may I introduce my colleagues, DCI Allan Mackay and DC Tim Myerscough."

Tim stood up and turned round. "Jessica?"

"I thought it was you, I just wanted to be sure. How are you? And how's you're crazy cousin?"

"Lucky's not my cousin, thank God, but well remembered."

"I never forget a pretty face," Jessica said.

"Would you two stop flirting and let this woman give me my meds?" Hunter grumbled. He looked up and saw Meera walk back into the ward. "Thank God you're back, darling. This nurse is conducting her love life and torturing me in the process."

"Probably no less than you deserve, Hunter." Meera smiled and handed out the coffees. "Now, shall we leave and let the nurse attend to the invalid?"

"I am an invalid already and I've still to have the operation on my wrist tomorrow."

Meera kissed Hunter on the forehead and she, Mackay and Tim left the ward.

"I'm going to hang on for a minute sir, I'll meet you at the car. Here are my keys."

Mackay looked heavenward. "Don't be long chatting up that nurse. I want those notes written up in time for a briefing at five o'clock."

Tim climbed into the driver's seat and put his coffee in the cup holder beside his knee. He noticed Mackay was holding his tightly, probably due to his impatience at getting kept waiting. Still, it was worth it, Jessica was off at Christmas and would be able to come to the party he had just decided to have.

"So how do you know the nurse, Myerscough?"

"She was working at the clinic where Lucky, sorry, Lord Lachlan Buchanan, was being treated for his addictions last year."

"Huh."

"It would seem she remembered me."

"Huh."

"I certainly remembered her."

"Huh. I thought you were dating Dr. Gillian Pearson. The one with the flash of green in her hair."

"I was, sir, but she's working abroad. I rarely hear from her now. I expect she's otherwise occupied."

"I expect she is. I know you certainly are. Report on my desk by four."

"Yes, sir." Tim grinned as he pulled into the station carpark.

Later when Tim walked into the incident room, he pulled up the chair next to Bear to tell him the good news.

"Since when did you have an annual Christmas party?" The big man laughed.

Mackay had a face like fizz as he slammed a folder on the desk to bring the briefing to order.

"Shut up! He shouted. "On top of everything else, we have had a report of a car stolen from Thomson's Top Cars by Mrs Claus. He glared around the room, daring any of the detectives to smile. When his glance fell on Mel Grant she couldn't hold it together and exploded with laughter.

"DC Grant, is theft funny?"

"No sir. Not at all, sir." She broke into renewed laughter and everybody in the room, including Mackay, joined in. Finally, he pulled himself together. "What is going on in this city?" He exclaimed. "Right, down to the serious business. First, DI Wilson. Will you start us off, DS Reid?"

Colin Reid stood up. "Nadia, I mean, DC Chan and I examined the CCTV records around the ATM at the West End and at the Castle Terrace car park.

"DI Wilson at the West End first, Reid. We'll get to the elf later."

"Fine. Yes, Nadia do you want to take this one?"

"Yep. We got the CCTV from the ATM itself, another recording from the Whisky place at the corner."

"Binns corner?"

"That's going back a bit, sir. But yes. And the CCTV from the Boots just along the street. We also approached the Job Centre because Hunter told you that one of the Santas complained the job only lasted six weeks and then they'd be back on benefits, but that wasn't any good, There have been forty-seven Santas and ninety-six elves hired in Edinburgh and Lothian over the Christmas period. It seems almost every store needs a Santa."

"Goodness! Who would believe it? Forty-seven," Mackay said.

"There were three of them, Hunter said, and there were only three stores in the city centre that hired three Santas. John Lewis, Debenhams, and Indices. We started with these."

"That's good thinking."

"Thank you sir." Nadia continued. "From the CCTV around the ATM we saw Hunter beside the Santas, and we could tell, comparing their height against his that one of the men was tall, probably six feet tall. Another was short. He didn't look any taller than I am, so about five feet four or five. The other one was really portly."

"He had a real Santa belly," Colin said.

"We could tell from the CCTV at the bank that all three of the men were involved in the crime, but we couldn't see their faces well enough to identify them." Nadia said. "However, when they ran away. The film from the Boots camera showed the short one ran East along Princes Street and the fat one waddled across the street. He jumped on a bus, but we couldn't see the number."

"Still, we know the stop and the time, so the bus company may be able to help," Colin said.

"Yes. Good. Where did the tall one go? Could you tell?" Mackay asked.

"We caught him on the Whisky place cameras, running West and around the corner into Queensferry Street. He jumped into a car parked on double yellow lines and drove away fast."

"Registration?"

"No sir, but we've got the make and colour, so we thought we'd check with the council if he got a ticket."

"Hmm. Yes, okay. Good start."

"Anyone got anything to add?"

"I checked with CSI," Bear said. "No DNA or fingerprints, and only DI Wilson's blood, so the scene of crime has been released.

"Much as I thought," Mackay said. "Still, we had to check."

"I'll leave it to DS Reid to see the reports are completed and to assign the outstanding tasks. I plan to get those bastards and ruin their Christmas."

"Now onto the elf." Mackay glared at Mel Grant and dared her to laugh. Mel lowered her head but Mackay could still see her shoulders shaking and her mop of dark curls bobbing up from a pizza box on a desk. "Hand me a slice of that, DC Grant and tell me what you discovered about the elf."

She nodded trying to keep her expression solemn as she handed the box over. She bit into her own slice of pizza so her mouth was full of pepperoni and grease. It gave her a moment to control herself. "Yes sir." She wiped her face on the tissue Bear handed to her. "Thanks, Bear."

"The elf, DC Grant, do we know his identity?" Mackay asked impatiently.

"No sir, but we're running his fingerprints through the system in case he's known to us."

"Fine."

"And Dr David Murray will be conducting the postmortem tomorrow. Dr Sharma flies out to India tomorrow to visit her family.

"Yes, Hunter was meant to be going. But that's not happening," Mackay said.

"No, of course sir. From the injuries Dr Murray noted on the corpse at the scene of crime, it seemed that the victim had been hit with a blunt instrument on the back of the head. There were also signs of bruising on his wrists."

"Hmm. Anything else?"

"Not that he could see, sir. The elf costume hid his body and the tights he was wearing covered his legs."

"Yes. Could he give you an approximate time of death?"

"Not there and then."

"You'd better attend the postmortem with DC Chan."

Nadia nodded. "Yes sir."

"What about me?" Bear asked.

"No Bear. On past performance, DC Chan is less likely to faint. CSI find anything?" Mackay asked Mel.

"They found a glove, a hammer and a large spanner under a car near the body. He had a phone on him too. These have been sent to forensics for examination, although they don't know if the tools or glove are anything to do with the death."

"He didn't have any ID on him?"

"No sir, but there were some blood spatters near his body. They've taken scrapings that will be examined to find out if they're the elf's blood. Apart from that it seemed clean. At least as clean as you'd expect a car park to be. There were also no surfaces that would take a fingerprint, except the call buttons for the lifts, but those have too much usage to be useful."

"Of course."

"The uniforms doing local interviews got a couple of witness statements,"

"Oh good, tell me Bear," Mackay said.

"A lawyer, Rosie French, was leaving her office late and saw a guy dressed as an elf running along towards the carpark about the right time, while a homeless man, Harry Marsh, told PC Neil Larkin that he saw Mrs Claus driving away from there, but he had no idea of the time. He said she almost ran over him in his sleeping bag."

"Mrs Claus could have been going to get help or running away from the scene of the crime." Bear said.

"Or there could be no connection at all," Nadia said. "it could all be coincidence."

"The boss doesn't like coincidences," Tim said.

"Neither do I." Mackay grumbled. "And why didn't we get a report of a car stolen by Mrs Claus from Thomson's Top Cars? Has nobody followed that up?" Mackay growled. "Right, I'll make sure we get the forensics and postmortem results tomorrow. In the meantime, DCs Myerscough and Zewedu, see what else Hunter recalls and stop by to interview Jamie Thomson about that stolen car. DCs Grant and Chan will attend the elf's postmortem. DS Reid and DC Anderson collate the reports from the CCTV and the witness statements, and we'll reconvene tomorrow."

Tim and Bear marched along the hospital corridor to Hunter's ward. They made an interesting duo; one tall with fair hair and broad shoulders, dressed in relaxed but expensive designer clothes, the other tall and black with equally wide shoulders and a more formal smart suit. When they arrived at Hunter's bedside, Meera Sharma had just risen to leave.

"Hi guys, I've told Meera she mustn't disappoint her family by staying here with me. Tell her. I'll be fine. There's nothing anybody can do until I get out of here, and it looks like that might be a couple of weeks. They haven't even operated on my wrist yet. It was too swollen."

Meera looked at Tim. "Look after him for me."

"I will."

She looked sternly at Bear. "Don't let him do anything stupid."

"Why do I always get the difficult jobs?"

The men grinned at Meera.

"Enjoy your holiday, darling, and send my love to each member of your crazy family," Hunter said.

"What do you mean they're crazy? They didn't get beaten up by Santa Claus." Meera kissed Hunter and left the ward.

"You are a lucky man, boss. What does she see in you?"

Hunter looked at his foot which was raised to keep his leg straight. "You're right Tim, I've been too scared to ask her, especially right now." He smiled. "Pull up a chair and tell me what you know."

"No boss, you're meant to tell us if you've remembered anything else," Bear said. "Would you recognise the men if you saw them again?"

"No chance, they were all dressed up and wore fake white

beards." Hunter paused. There can't be that many stores near the city centre hiring Santas can there?"

"Forty-seven Santas hired in the area, and ninety-six elves but only three stores hired three Santas to provide cover in shifts. Uniforms are going to interview the relevant store managers."

"Elves!" Hunter exclaimed. "One of the Santas, the tallest one, said they'd had they're tips stolen by an elf. He said he'd like to kill him." Hunter moved and then grimaced in pain.

"That's interesting, because a guy dressed as an elf has been found dead in Castle Terrace car park," Tim said.

"And Mrs Claus stole a car from Thomson's Top Cars," said Bear.

"Look, I can't do anything about this here, but there's something strange with all this. Could you find the connection for me? There must be one."

"Must be one what, Hunter?" Ailsa Myerscough asked as she walked in. "Don't get him too excited, Tim. I'm going to operate on that wrist later." She smiled at Tim and Bear. "Staff nurse Jessica will be along to take you for premeds and so on shortly Hunter. Is there anything you want to ask?"

"Will I die?"

"It's always a risk, but probably not. As I said, boys, no excitement." Then, as quietly as she had arrived, Ailsa left to carry on with her work.

"If there's nothing else you can tell us, we're off to see Jamie and Frankie at Thomson's Top Cars," Bear said. "We'll do our best to find out what's going on."

"I don't want your best. I just want you to solve these crimes. There's too much Christmas in them for my liking."

The staff nurse walked towards them. "We still on for that Christmas Eve party, Tim?"

"Yes of course, I'm looking forward to it."

"Good. Me too. It's such a nice tradition to have one every year."

Bear looked heavenward.

"I'm glad you think so." Tim blushed.

"Now, you boys better leave. I'm sorry to break up this little chat but Mr Wilson here is going to spend some time with Ms Myerscough. Here we go, Hunter." She moved the brakes on the bed and pushed it expertly towards the lifts.

"Have you done anything about arranging this 'annual' party?" Bear asked.

"Not a thing. Will you and Mel come?"

"Of course. I'll even bring beer. Now, Thomson's Top Cars?" Bear asked Tim.

"Lead the way, big man!"

"Hello Blondie!" Jamie Thomson shouted across the showroom to Tim. "And if your pal is here to tell me that the lovely DC Grant has thrown him over for lust of me, tell him she's too late, I'm spoken for."

"You're a funny guy, Jamie," Bear said.

"He likes to think so." Frankie Hope, Jamie's cousin, walked behind Tim and Bear as he came in from the garage.

"Sorry to disappoint you Jamie. We've come to talk to you about Mrs Claus and your stolen car." Tim smiled.

"It's a bloody pain. Frankie saw her too. Want a coffee?" Jamie asked.

"Yes please."

"Frankie, Blondie wants a coffee. Can you make them?"

"What did your last slave die of?"

"Hard work!" The cousins spoke at the same time and laughed.

"How'd you take it?" Frankie asked. After acknowledging the replies, he sloped off to make the drinks.

Jamie led the way to the office.

"I wouldn't have believed it if Frankie hadn't seen it too. But we were just closing up and bringing the cars in from the forecourt. The phone rang and I dodged in to get it."

"He left the keys in the car, didn't he? If that had been me I'd have got a right bollocking." Frankie came in with a tray full of coffees and a packet of Jaffa Cakes.

"Not the good biscuits Frankie. What are you thinking?"

Tim laughed.

"It's Christmas." Frankie shrugged and set the tray on the desk. He grabbed a mug, opened the biscuits and, with a defiant stare at Jamie, took one and offered the packet to Tim.

"We appreciate your sacrifice, Jamie," Tim said helping himself to two Jaffa Cakes and passing the packet to Bear.

Jamie sighed.

"So you saw the woman steal the car?" Bear asked.

"Yes, but not up close. She must have been standing watching us from somewhere. By the time she was in view on the forecourt, I was at the front desk on the phone."

"Over there?" Tim pointed to the reception desk.

Jamie nodded. "Yes."

"I was polishing the red car there." Frankie pointed to a red Porsche. "So I wasn't that close to her either. Anyway, she was dressed up as Santa's wife."

"So what can you remember about her?" Bear asked.

"Nice legs." Frankie grinned.

"Aye smashing pins." Jamie agreed. "But she'd a grey curly wig on."

"You're sure it was a wig?" Tim asked.

"Yes. Nobody wears their hair like that. And her hair underneath was black."

"Black? Not brown."

"I said black."

"Okay. What else?"

"Bright red tights, a short green and red dress and a silly hat."

"What about gloves? Was she wearing gloves?"

"I don't remember. I was on the phone. But there was something familiar about her. And she was short."

"Aye, little." Frankie agreed with his cousin and held his hand out to indicate someone about five feet tall.

"Hmm. That's little." Bear agreed. "What did you do when you saw the car move away?"

"I dropped the phone and yelled at her to fucking stop."

"The polish hit the deck and I ran after her, but she was too fast. Then we called your guys." Frankie tried to sneak another Jaffa Cake but stopped in his tracks as Jamie scowled at him. "Nobody came."

"That was yesterday the car could be in France by now." Jamie complained.

"But we don't think it is. A Mrs Claus was seen driving into the Castle Terrace carpark yesterday evening."

"I heard about a dead body found there," Frankie said.

"Yes, that's right. There might be a connection. We're trying to get a decent enough photo from CCTV to get you to identify her."

"In a Christmas fancy dress costume? I can't see that helping much." Jamie scoffed.

"I know, but we've got to start somewhere. Can you give us the make and model of the car. Colour, registration that sort of thing."

"Yep. We can do that," Jamie said. He pulled up the details on the computer in front of him and printed the page off. "There you go, Blondie. Find the car before I have to tell me pop it's missing, will you?"

"I'll do my best. How is your dad, anyway, Jamie?"

"Oh, you know, another festive season in the clink. He's just living the dream."

Nadia drove to the mortuary. She had been there more often than Mel and knew the way. At this time of year there were decorations in the windows they passed and lights on the trees in the Grass Market as they drove along. It made the journey bright as they approached their destination. Nevertheless, as they crossed the junction towards the canyon of old, black buildings on the immediate approach to the Edinburgh City Mortuary, the road was dark in the winter afternoon and made her shudder. This street seemed foreboding, even in summer; in winter it was worse.

The building was situated in the part of Edinburgh known as the Cowgate. The area derived its name from the historic practice of herding cattle down the street on market days. Nadia looked into the Cowgate and thought what a narrow road it was, only one lane wide in each direction. She stared at the steep gradients leading off to either side. Nadia glanced at Mel and noticed she was frowning. There was nowhere obvious to park, so she lurched the car around and Mel gripped on to the handle of the car door as she swung into the car park and drew up at the rear beside the anonymous black 'private ambulances' outside the morgue.

Mel's silence throughout the journey had done nothing to make it more pleasant for Nadia but she understood that Mel was dreading the postmortem and wouldn't be here if she could have avoided it. They arrived early, so sat in the car for a few minutes.

"Imagine dressing up as an elf to make children happy and getting killed for it," Mel said.

"I doubt that's why he was killed."

"Well being murdered in that stupid outfit. It's horrible."

"Being murdered is the bad bit," Nadia said.

"Yes, I suppose it is. Meera's already away, isn't she?"

"I think she leaves tonight. She's flying East so it's probably an overnight flight. I wonder how long it takes to fly to India. It's about thirteen hours to Beijing."

"Furthest East I've been is Turkey. Me and Bear went to Antalya. Great holiday that was."

"I doubt Meera'll have much of a holiday. She'll spend all her time worrying about the boss."

"I was surprised she went," Mel said. "David Murray's doing the postmortem."

"Probably. with Aiden, what's his name?"

"Fraser. It's Aiden Fraser," Mel said.

"Thanks. That's right. We better go in now, I suppose." Nadia got out of the car first and entered the building in front of Mel.

Aiden scrubbed up and disinfected his hands then made his way over to the examination room where David Murray was already waiting for him. He had wheeled in the body of the elf and had already transferred it to a stainless-steel table that occupied the middle of the spotlessly clean white floor. The elf was lying on his back with his arms loosely resting by his sides.

Aiden glanced at David and shook his head. "This is so sad. Imagine losing someone to a violent death this close to Christmas," he said.

"Yes, and so very difficult for his family. Do we know who they are?"

"I haven't been told." Aiden said. "I wonder who will join us today from amongst Scotland's finest?"

"Nadia Chan?" David suggested. "The rest of the team don't have the stomach for a postmortem, from what we've seen."

Aiden nodded. He turned his attention to the body on the table. He noted the livor mortis on the man's body caused by the settling of the blood. "He was definitely killed in the location where he was found."

David frowned. "Yes indeed. Oh, it sounds like the boys in blue are arriving. Sorry, girls in blue." He smiled as Nadia and Mel entered the examination room.

Nadia was amazed, as always, how much it resembled an operating theatre.

Aiden looked up and smiled at Nadia. "DC Chan, DC Grant, thank you for coming. It seems we guessed correctly, David, when we thought Nadia would be one of our observers. Always good to see you again, Nadia. You are becoming Edinburgh's go-to girl for postmortems."

"That's an accolade I'll gladly go without," Mel said. She wrinkled her nose as she breathed in the distinctive smell of the cold air.

"It's always interesting, but I would happily never come here again if it meant that people stopped getting hurt," Nadia looked at the floor then spoke quietly to Mel. "We should get gowned up."

"You lead the way, Nadia. There really is an odd smell in here, isn't there?"

"Yes, a bit like a combination of formaldehyde, antiseptic and industrial soap, isn't it? It's also a bit chilly, just those few degrees below what would be considered comfortable makes all the difference," Nadia said.

When Mel and Nadia returned to witness the postmortem, Mel commented, "I've never been here before. It's quite a big room, isn't it?"

"Yes, well by the time I've got my large double sinks along the wall, a metal counter to hold all the tools and the channel leading to the drain, I suppose it has to be big," Aiden said.

"Shall we get on?" David asked.

The two DCs moved so that they could see the body on the stainless-steel examination table below the powerful circular halogen lights which were suspended from the ceiling.

"He's quite a short man," Mel said.

"True." Aiden positioned himself on the other side of the table from the two detectives. He measured the man's height. "Five feet three inches tall."

"That's shorter than I am," Mel said.

They watched in silence as the doctor freed the body from its curl-toed slippers and tights. There were holes in the tights where the elf had probably tripped trying to escape in the ridiculous outfit. His knees and one of his shins were cut and grazed. Aiden also commented on abrasions and colour changes to the elf's ankles.

"David, look at this," he said. "His ankles were held or

restrained in some way, by the looks of things." David pulled a face as he watched Aiden remove the rest of the elf's outfit. "There's bits of dirt stuck to that," he said.

"Probably from when he struggled to try to make his escape," David said.

After the pieces of clothing were cut from the body, Aiden gave them to David. He put each item carefully into plastic evidence bags which would be handed over to the forensics experts for further examination. Aiden then took blood, urine, and hair samples as well as oral and anal swabs.

"Look at this, David," he said. "He's been hit hard, but not right at the back of the head, it's slightly to the left-hand side."

"Nasty!" David Murray frowned. "But from the site and look of that wound my guess is that the attacker was standing behind him. I think the assailant was tall and probably left-handed. Would you agree, Aiden?"

"They wouldn't have to be very tall; this fellow is only five foot three, remember. But only about ten percent of the population is left-handed, so that may help our detectives."

Aiden used a pair of safety scissors to cut open the elf's boxers. As he pulled them off, his eyes slowly ran up and down the elf's torso.

"He must have dropped onto the ground hard when he was hit. Look how bruised his hips are. It differs from the lividity caused by the pooling of blood after death. This was a violent assault."

Nadia gasped. "That is so mean. He's only little."

"But somebody was determined to rid the world of him," Mel said. "I wonder what he did."

"It doesn't matter, Mel. He didn't deserve such a violent death." Nadia took her colleague to task.

"Of course, you're right." Mel agreed.

David reached for the digital camera and documented everything as Aiden finished examining the body. He sprayed it with fungicide and used a hose with a powerful water jet to methodically wash and disinfect the corpse fully. When he was finished, Aiden checked that the directional light in his headset was switched on and turned on his voice recorder. He dictated the official examination. He began by stating the date and time, followed by the case number then described the general state of the body, before moving on to describe the grisly details.

"No other suspicious bruises," David commented.

A touch check of the elf's neck revealed that neither his larynx nor his trachea had collapsed. "His thyroid bone in her neck isn't fractured, so there's nothing to suggest that he was strangled either," Aiden said, glancing at David.

He then turned his attention back to the elf's body and checked for signs of sexual molestation or any other kind of aggression. He began with the mouth, pulling it open and checking for any trauma or skin and teeth colour alteration in case a poison had been used that discoloured the teeth or tongue or perhaps burned the skin inside her mouth. Aiden found no primary indications of poisoning, but a toxicology report would be instructed anyway.

Aiden undertook to have his report with Nadia the following day. He didn't want to leave it any closer to the Christmas festivities.

"It's been a while since we partnered up, Rachael. I seem to remember you drink chamomile tea?"

"Yes, please."

Colin got up from his chair. "What is the appeal of drinking hot wet straw?"

"It keeps me calm."

"If you need to keep calm, you're in the wrong job." Colin walked across the room towards the kettle. "You still fancy a change to VSO?"

"Victim Support Officer, yes. I think I'd be good at that."

When he returned with her tea, Rachael saw he'd brought nothing for himself. "What are you having?!

"I've got a refillable bottle, I just fill it with water from the tap and I've got a squeezy lemon to put a few drops in, for when I need sweetening up."

Rachael smiled. "Do you want to start collating the CCTV or the witness statements?"

"Nadia and I have been through the CCTV already. Why don't you start with that, and see if you find anything we missed? I'll start with the witness statements."

"Let's do that." Rachael sipped her tea and turned to her computer. She brought up the file and started examining what they had. "The boss didn't half go down with a clatter didn't he?"

"Yeh and missing his trip to India with Meera. That's a shame. He doesn't take many holidays."

"Ooh, Colin, did you and Nadia notice a fellow dressed as an elf getting out of the car with the three Santas? Look, he's standing in that shop doorway but the three Santas who attacked the boss have walked away. The timing looks like it's just before the boss was attacked."

"No, let me see." Colin got up from his chair and walked over to Rachael's computer. "Hmm. I wonder what he's up to. Run it back a bit."

They stared at the film and followed the elf as he went into the Oddbins liquor store and then went back to the car. He tried the handle of the door to no avail.

"He's got a carrier bag in his hand. Look!" They watched as the elf sauntered back along Queensferry Street towards the large pub on the corner.

"Can you read that number plate on the car from this angle?" Colin asked.

"FS57 maybe. No, I can't be sure, it's just not clear enough."

They continued to watch as the elf walked back along the street. They lost sight of him after he went into Ryan's Bar.

"Well, there can't have been that many elves drinking in the pub that evening," Colin said. "Shall we go and see what anybody remembers?"

After showing their ID the manager introduced herself as Beverley Ann Hopper and led them to her office.

"You can call me Bev," she said. "How can I help?" she asked.

"We're investigating an incident that happened a couple of nights ago," Colin said.

"Was that when that guy got mugged in Princes Street?"

"Yes, that's it," Rachael said.

"Bloody shame. But it was at the bank, not here."

"That's right, but did you notice a short man come in here? He was probably quite obvious; he was dressed as an elf."

Beverley laughed. "I'm so glad I was on duty, otherwise I wouldn't have believed it. Yes, he came in. We had Mrs Claus here too – it was hilarious, until it turned nasty. Please take a seat."

"Thank you," Colin said.

Beverley led the way. "So what do you want to know about the elf on the shelf?"

Rachael looked puzzled.

"Well, he was so short he looked like he was sitting on a shelf when he clambered up onto a bar stool. We couldn't hardly see him when he stood at the bar. We all had a bit of a laugh."

Colin couldn't help smiling at Bev, she had such a cheerful demeanour. "Sadly the man who was dressed as the elf was killed that same night at the carpark on Castle Terrace."

"I'm sorry, but I can't say I'm surprised. What an obnoxious little toerag he was. Pushed past other customers, cursed at my staff. I don't think he was drunk, but he was horrible. Vulgar to one of the girls clearing tables too. There's no need for that.

"He was rude to one of the customers too." Beverley looked over to Colin. "This woman was sitting alone. She had a red coat on and a grey wig. I noticed she was wearing a Mrs Santa costume underneath her coat. We get a lot of fancy dress this time of year, you know office parties and so on."

Rachael nodded. "Did the elf go and sit with that woman?"

"No, quite the opposite. He shouted across something like, 'I bet your knockers aren't real, and neither's your hair, you queer.' And she looked so upset. She just finished her drink and left, the people at the next table commented to the server about his language. The woman hadn't been doing any harm."

"Could you describe Mrs Claus to us?" Colin asked.

"Not really. She wore a lot of makeup, you know, mascara, bright red lipstick and her cheeks were painted to make them look rosy."

Bev directed this description to Rachael. "I mean, it was obvious she was wearing a wig, but I couldn't tell you what colour her real hair was. And although she had a thick coat, her legs were slim, so I don't think she was a big woman. You know?

"Anyway, shortly after that, the elf left too. I was glad to see the back of him. He'd only have caused trouble if he'd stayed," Bev said. "I can do without that at this time of year."

"What happened?" Colin asked.

"He stood up, swore, finished his pint, and left, announcing that he had other places to be. Everybody in the pub cheered and he stormed out."

"Did you see which way he went?"

"No sorry, love, I have no idea. We were right busy. I was just glad to see him go."

"What time would that be?"

"I can't say exactly. We'd had our evening rush in between five and seven o'clock. He probably left around eight, because I was going on my break."

"Do you have CCTV here?" Colin asked.

"Yes, but I don't have time to sit with you. If I get it loaded up for you, can you manage?"

"I'm sure we can, Bev, Colin here is a past master in working CCTV machines."

"Mrs Claus did leave this." Bev handed Rachael a half-eaten sausage roll. "It looks like it comes from Greggs. They're not meant to eat food in here that they don't buy from us. I kept it to remind the staff to take punters to task if they find them munching on something like this. I know it's cheaper, but I've got a business to run."

"That's excellent, Bev. We'll take that and see what forensics can tell us," Colin said.

"I didn't think you were going to eat it!" the manager laughed. "Come on, I'll set up the CCTV for you."

When they had finished watching the film of the elf's pub visit, Colin and Rachael arranged with Bev that she would come into the station the following day to give a statement.

"That was a good spot, Rachael. It gives us the time period for the elf getting to the car park."

"But funny he left without his booze. If he was bad tempered in the pub before then, he'd have been furious when he realised he'd left his drink behind."

"There were no bottles found at the carpark, so it doesn't look like he went back for it. Or maybe the killer nicked his drink too. Let's stop into Oddbins and see if they can help us. A wee guy dressed as an elf might just be someone they'd remember. Then we can toss a coin for who writes the report."

Rachael lost.

When Hunter came round from his surgery he was aching all over and hungry enough to eat a scabby dog. He felt for his buzzer and then opened his eyes. Tim and Bear were sitting talking quietly with Ailsa.

"Don't you have anything better to do than watch me sleep? Get something to help me with pain, Ailsa? And I need to eat."

"My goodness, this is some charm offensive." Ailsa smiled. She stuck a

thermometer into Hunter's mouth and held his uninjured wrist to take his pulse. She waited a few moments, then took the thermometer out and examined it.

"Apart from being a grumpy bugger, how is he, sis?" Tim asked.

"He'll live. I'll get him some tea and toast and ask Jessie to sort out his pain, then I'll have to get back to work, my break's almost over."

"I am here you know." Hunter complained.

"Oh, yes, we know, boss. How does Meera sleep? You snore like a bull." Bear grinned.

"I do not snore, you're a cheeky bastard, Zewedu."

Ailsa left to make the arrangements she had spoken about and shortly afterwards Jessie arrived to administer the necessary pain killers.

"So why are you here and not working?" Hunter asked Tim and Bear.

"We are working, boss and we came to tell you what we know. I think you may be able to help us."

"Oh aye, can't even cope with a bloody assault without me now?"

"We think your assault might be connected to a murder in Castle Terrace car park." Bear pulled his chair closer to Hunter and spoke softly. "This is the timeline. You were attacked about five thirty, boss."

"Yes, I suppose. We left the travel agent not long before close of business; Meera went back to finish packing and I walked around to draw money in Princes Street."

"A bloke dressed as an elf went into Ryan's on the corner fifteen minutes later, boss," Tim said. "He had travelled with the three Santas who attacked you to the West End, but he went to the off licence then the pub while the Santas went to draw money like you did."

"You know I was actually trying to be nice and give them a few quid for a pint because they were arguing about who should pay for their drinks." Hunter sounded aggrieved and frowned. He moved to try to get more comfortable. "This leg makes it impossible to rest easy. If I'd known they were going to go for me, I wouldn't have bothered."

"Who was it said, 'No good deed goes unpunished?'" Bear asked.

"Oscar Wilde." Tim replied.

"It's always Oscar Wilde, Shakespeare or Churchill."

"Yes, it usually is Bear." Hunter nodded. "Do you know who any of these characters are yet."

"No. But we have the list of local Santas working in the city centre and we've got the list down to three groups of three. I wondered if you could take a look at it." Tim tied to hand the list of names to Hunter.

"Just read it to me young Myerscough."

"You might know of any bad apples who had been released recently and might have taken the short-term work." Bear looked over Tim's shoulder at the list. "That name sounds familiar." Hunter commented as Tim reached the middle name in the middle group.

"Give it here, Tim." Hunter squinted at the list. "I know all the names, but I thought he was still inside and that one was in Costa del Crime last I heard. He must be back."

"Apparently so. Is that guy one of the notorious Flamingo family?" Tim asked.

"Well thought, young Myerscough. Flamingos because their surname is Bird and they're tall with skinny legs. Now I think about it, the tall one could have been old Jock Bird. Bastard."

"Didn't his wife fly off with Shady Peckham's son?"

"Ha ha, Bear. Boss, we'll take a look at what we've got at the briefing this afternoon and let you know tomorrow."

"Aye, fine Tim. God, I'm so bloody tired. I'll have to let you go, lads."

"Anaesthetic takes it out of you. Anything you need, boss?" Bear asked.

"Food and sleep, but not necessarily in that order."

Mackay banged a file on the desk in front of him. Why did briefing rooms always smell of coffee? He looked around and saw most of the team had mugs in their hands. He smiled. That would do it.

Tim walked in and put a box of 12 Krispy Kreme doughnuts on the table in the middle of the room. Bear grabbed two and most of the rest of the team were hovering about. Only Colin Reid ignored the treats and chomped on an apple. Mackay decided to get his hand in to take a chocolate one before calling the room to order.

He smiled at Tim and waved the cake in his general direction by way of thanks. The young DC nodded back.

"Okay!" Mackay made himself heard above the rumble of conversations. "What do we have and what do we know?" He looked around the room.

"I think we may have had a breakthrough, sir," Colin said. "Rachael noticed a bit more activity around the car that the three Santas got out of. There was also a fellow dressed as an elf sitting in the front passenger seat. Nadia and I missed him, because he was very small and almost hidden by the fat Santa."

"Is it our elf?" Mackay asked.

"I don't know, but we know a bit about how he spent his evening."

"We know from the CCTV footage that the car was a Ford Escort. Witnesses said it was bright red, like the Santa costumes."

Everybody groaned at Rachael. It was such a popular make of car.

"Yes, but we have a partial registration number."

Colin looked at her quizzically.

"Yes we do, Colin. It was in the witness statement from two of the people at the bus stop. It began SS. One fellow said he remembered that because it was his initials, Scott Sanderson and the other man waiting for a bus was an off-duty traffic warden and said he'd have loved to book three Santas this close to Christmas for parking on a double yellow line. He thought the number was SS67 but he wasn't sure about the numbers."

"SS is a Dundee registration," Mackay frowned. "See what you can find from DVLA, Rachael."

"I've already made the call, sir. They'll get back to me today."

"Colin, you said you knew how this elf had spent his time?"

"Yes. Rachael spotted this again. When he got out of the car, he went to Oddbins, the off-licence in Queensferry Street. Then he went into Ryan's Bar on the corner. The manageress was very helpful."

"She remembered him then Colin?"

"Oh yes, sir. Largely because he was an obnoxious little tyke and struggled to get a perch on the bar stool."

Tim laughed.

"Not a problem you'd be familiar with, Tim" Colin said.

"No but it paints a funny picture."

"She said he was there until almost eight o'clock. She remembered because she was just about to go on her break. But as the elf was becoming increasingly vulgar. He picked a fight with a woman dressed as Mrs Santa too. The manageress didn't know anything about the attack on Hunter, she thought it most likely they were going to a Christmas themed fancy dress party. The elf left after he finished his pint. There were complaints about his language from other customers."

"So he left without any more trouble?"

"Yes, but Bev, the manageress, didn't see where he went."

"Pity. Did she describe Mrs Santa?"

"Sort of. She said she was a thin woman with bright red lipstick, heavy mascara, and a grey wig."

"So all she needs to do is wash her face and take her wig off and we have a skinny woman."

"Well, not quite, boss. Bev found the woman had been eating a sausage roll that she hadn't bought from the pub. So we have that." Rachael looked round in triumph.

"Why did she keep a half-eaten sausage roll?" Bear asked.

"To do a training reminder with her staff." Colin explained. "We sent it for urgent analysis in the hope Mrs Claus's DNA might be on record.

"Brilliant. That's what we need. And you've been through the CCTV?" Mackay asked Colin.

"Yes, sir. I downloaded the relevant periods, so we have that."

"Good. What about the stuff the elf bought in Oddbins. Did the CSIs find it near his body?" Mackay asked.

"There wasn't any booze found around the crime scene, so he may have left it in the pub, or it got stolen after he was attacked." Colin added.

"He really didn't have a good day," Mackay said. "Did he use a card to pay."

"Cash in the pub. But Colin and I did go over to speak to the manager at Oddbins. He remembered the elf and identified him from his post-mortem photo. Said he's a regular, Graham Crosbie. Lives down Fountain Bridge but doesn't want to share his drink with his flatmate so he buys it there on his way home and hides it in his room."

"Funny. Sounds like you, Bear." Mel winked.

"So we have a name for our victim. Card payment this time?"

"Cash again. But he has a loyalty card that he always swipes. Confirms his name. Address, on the card, 115 Fountainbridge."

"Can you and Colin get round there when we're finished?"

"Uniform is already on their way. PS Charlie Middleton and PC Neil Larkin."

"Hmm, I don't much rate Charlie's bedside manner, so I hope it's not a grieving parent he finds there. Okay, DC Anderson. Thanks."

Rachael blushed and bit her lip.

"How did the post-mortem go, DC Chan?"

Nadia explained all that they had learned from Dr Aiden Fraser earlier and told Mackay that the report would be with them tomorrow.

"Wants it off his desk before Christmas, then."

Nadia smiled. "I'd guess so, sir. I would if I were him."

"So would I. Now how did the big men get on at Thomson's Top Cars?" Mackay turned his attention to Tim and Bear.

"We met with Jamie and Frankie. They both saw Mrs Santa and, apart from admiring her legs, were useless at telling us what she looked like. Oh, and Mel, don't be too heart-broken, but Jamie says you've missed your chance with him. He's spoken for." Bear smiled.

"And a Merry Christmas to you too, Mr Zewedu. That's one thing I can cross off my list of worries."

"What could they tell you about the car?" Mackay asked. He didn't want the meeting to stray off topic.

"They were spot on about that," Tim said. "They printed this off for us." He handed round copies of the details Jamie had printed off. "It's a black Volvo V40."

"A Volvo? How on earth did the woman steal that?"

"Jamie was bringing the newer cars from the forecourt into the showroom for the close of business, but when the phone rang he left the keys on the ignition."

"Fuck's sake," Mel said.

"My thoughts precisely, DC Grant," Mackay said. "Registration according to this is SK63 XOX"

"Yes, sir. We've circulated the description of the car and registration." Tim paused. "We didn't bother with a description of the driver, because we thought she'd just take her wig off and immediately look different."

"We've said it was a woman driver, last seen wearing a Mrs Claus Christmas costume, but I doubt it'll be much use."

"Agreed, DC Zewedu. Were they able to give us anything else that might be helpful?" Mackay asked.

"Yes, sir, it might well be. Jamie told us they'd been doing some work on the car and there was a hammer and a large spanner on the passenger seat. He was going to take it back to the mechanics that work for him when he brought the car in," Bear said.

"The CSIs found a hammer and a spanner near the corpse, didn't they? If they have fingerprints on them, that might be useful. I don't suppose we know how Mrs Claus paid in the pub?"

"No sir," Rachael shook her head.

"Without that, we don't know if it's the same woman. Unless we can get DNA off the spanner or hammer and the sausage roll. That sausage roll is a Godsend."

"It's what I always say about Greggs' sausage rolls, sir."

"Shut up, Zewedu. Now tomorrow, I want DS Reid and DC Chan to go through the CCTV footage again and home in on any frames that may help identify the attackers."

Colin and Nadia nodded and smiled at each other.

"DC Anderson." Mackay turned his attention to Rachael. "You chase forensics. I want their report. Oh, and make sure DVLA do their bit. I don't want them to close for the festive with our Santas' car stuck in their computer."

"Yes, sir."

"DC Grant," Mackay said. Mel looked up. "When that post-mortem report comes in you must make a note of the salient points for the team. And get statements from PS Charlie Middleton and PC Neil Larkin about their visit to the elf's home."

"Yes, sir."

"Myerscough and Zewedu, find out about the lists of three Santas. Pay each of them a visit and let's see who we can eliminate."

"Do you want us to visit at home or at work, sir?" Bear asked.

"Do I look like a man who cares? Just get it done. We'll debrief with our updated information tomorrow. One of our own is in hospital and we have a dead body on our patch. Let's get the buggers who did this and ruin the festive period for them."

. . .

Hunter struggled up the stairs to his office. This fucking building should have a lift that worked. It had been out of order for at least three months with no sign that it was going to be fixed any time soon. Damn! Every step shot pain through his body. He'd never felt pain like it. Maybe Ailsa had been right, and he shouldn't have discharged himself. But he couldn't just sit around doing nothing, could he? A man was dead, and he wanted to catch the bastards who had mugged him before Christmas.

When he finally made it to his door, he was surprised to find it open. Bear stood by his coffee machine ladling some of his fresh Colombian coffee into his machine.

"Help yourself, DC Zewedu," Hunter said. He watched Bear jump and coffee granules flew all over the window ledge.

"What the fuck are you doing here?" Bear asked.

"I might ask you the same thing, Bear. After all, this is my office and that is my coffee."

"Bloody hell, boss. What are you doing here?" Tim stood at the door behind Hunter. "Ailsa said last night you'd be in hospital until after Christmas."

"I am here because this is my office and it would appear that Ms Myerscough was wrong."

"Isn't your leg sore? And your wrist?"

"I've never felt pain like it young Myerscough. I think the morphine is wearing off. But Bear here was just about to make me some coffee, would you two like some too?"

"Thanks boss. We just thought your coffee wouldn't stay fresh until after Christmas, so we should use it up."

"So you did, Bear." Hunter grinned. "Anyway, enough! When is the briefing due to start and is there anything I should know about?"

"Now boss. I'm sure there'll be a great deal for you to catch up on. Do you want me to carry you through? Bear can bring the coffee."

"Oh preserve my dignity. Just open the fucking door, Tim."

Tim held the door of the briefing room open to allow Hunter to negotiate his way into the room with as little difficulty as possible. Every member of the team looked up and gasped.

Nadia Chan got out of her chair and turned it around to offer the seat to Hunter, Colin stopped chomping his apple and stared open mouthed, but it was DCI Allan Mackay who broke the silence.

"For the love of all that is holy, what in buggeration are you doing here, man?"

"Good to see you too, sir." Hunter grimaced as he sat down, "I thought I might be able to help get my assault and the elf's death put to bed before Christmas, if that's all right with you."

"Huh. I doubt you'll be anything more than a liability in that state, but let's see." Mackay shook his head. Let's start at the beginning. Reid, Chan, anything new on the CCTV?"

"No sir, but we did get a good image of Graham Crosbie as he came out of Oddbins. They have a lot of attempted shopliftings especially at this time of year, so they have a camera that takes a photo of every customer as they leave the shop. It helps to identify any light-fingered customers." Colin finished speaking and turned to Nadia.

"We also got a good image of Mrs Claus as she drove into the Castle Terrace carpark. Each driver is snapped as they take their ticket."

"But that doesn't tell us if it was the same Mrs Santa as was in the pub arguing with our elf. Maybe the manager would recognise her. Any news from forensics, DC Anderson?"

"Not yet, sir."

"I'll go and chivvy them up," Hunter said. He stood up. "I might as well put my agony to good use. It might guilt-trip them into putting us at the top of the queue. Tim, can you get the doors for me and pour me another coffee?"

"Yes, boss." Tim paused. "Before you go, you might want to know that DS Charlie Middleton got his report typed up. It transpires that our elf, Graham Crosbie, lived with his stepfather, Sandy Brodie."

"Brodie, that name's familiar. Mostly drunk and disorderlies if I recall. Did they speak to him?" Hunter sat down again and adjusted his position on the chair.

"No, but a nosy neighbour wanted to find out why two pigs were hanging around their stair. Neil Larkin said Charlie told her the pigs were snuffling through rubbish for their Christmas dinner."

"Trust bloody Charlie."

"Neil managed to get her to laugh with him and talk about the neighbours. She said, father and son had regular huge arguments. Usually about money or booze, but they'd been calmer recently when they both got jobs at Indices on Princes Street working as Santa and an elf over the Christmas period."

"Good for Neil."

"Apparently she told him they were noisy neighbours, but she was too scared to confront them because Brodie was a nasty fat bastard."

"She's right there."

"They usually got home about seven at night, but she hadn't heard them since Wednesday. Quiet as the grave, she said."

"That might be right too. But even if Graham is dead, where's Brodie and why didn't he report his stepson missing?" Hunter stood up again. "I'm going to call forensics."

Tim stood up too and easily got to the door before Hunter. He picked up their mugs and Bear handed him another. Tim smiled and moved speedily along the corridor to get Hunter settled in his office with his phone, and mug on the side of his good arm, before returning to the briefing with coffee for Bear and himself.

"Is Crosbie on the database?" Mackay asked Nadia.

"No, sir. Now that we have a name for the stepfather I'll check him."

"Yes good. Do we have names of the other Santas working with Brodie?"

Tim checked his notes. "Yes, sir. The three working for Indices were Sandy Brodie, Ian Brown and Mike Bird."

"Bird, that name rings a bell. I had a run in with a whole family of Birds as a young copper. But it wasn't Michael." Mackay paused and raised his eyes. "I think it was Jock Bird who was head of the family. Nasty, wiry man sneaky as a snake and as much patience as a rhino. He'd be a right old man, if he's still alive, but I wonder if it's the same family. He was bad news."

"What about Mrs Claus? Did anywhere employ women to act as her?"

Tim looked down at his notes again. "There were only four people employed as Mrs Santa, so far as we know in the central Edinburgh area. John Lewis, Debenhams, and Indices again and The City of Edinburgh Council hired a Santa Claus, Mrs Claus and two elves to work at the Castle from eleven in the morning until four in the afternoon."

"The timings for the castle are too early, I think. Our investigation deals with actions taken in line with shop hours," Mackay said.

Tim nodded his agreement. "Jamie and Frankie said the Mrs Claus who stole a car from them had black hair, "

"They were insistent it was black, not brown," Bear said. He looked over Tim's shoulder. "The Mrs Claus employed by Indices was called Inaya Khan. I don't want to racially profile, but the chances are good that this lady has black hair."

Tim felt his phone vibrate in his pocket. He pulled it out and glanced at it. "The boss wants to come back. I'll go and open the doors for him."

"Yes do that," Mackay said. "DC Chan and DC Grant, do we have the post-mortem report from Dr Fraser yet?"

"No, sir."

"Go and chase it, will you DC Grant?"

Mel followed Tim out of the room. "I couldn't believe it when the boss was back this morning. How do you think he got up the stairs?

"Slowly, painfully and with determination, DC Grant." Hunter stood at the door of his office holding the door but unable to move further without knocking himself over until Tim helped him.

"Yes, boss." Mel ran along the corridor to her desk to make the phone call.

As Hunter and Tim re-entered the briefing room, Colin and Rachael were explaining to the team all they had learned from Bev Hopper.

"She's an observant woman. Thank goodness she kept that half-eaten sausage roll," Mackay said. "It could be very important."

"It is sir. Very important, but that's not all."

"Go on, DC Grant." Mackay looked at Mel sternly.

"Graham Crosbie died from the blow to the back of the head. The heavy implement used was the big spanner found beside him."

"How can Dr Fraser be so sure of that?" Hunter asked.

"He didn't know it was that spanner, but he knew it was a spanner because of the distinctive dent it left in Graham's skull"

Hunter pulled a face. "Could be," he said.

Mel caught her breath and carried on. "But what ties it up is the forensics report. That came through from the lab as I was passing. An effort had been made to wipe the spanner clean, but there were traces of Graham's blood and brains all over it and the boffins found enough DNA and fingerprints to identify who used it last."

"Please don't tell me it was Jamie Thomson," Tim groaned.

"His were there, but not to the same extent as the last person."

"Are you going to tell us, or do we have to guess?" Colin asked.

"I'd love you to guess but you'll never get it in a million years."

"DC Grant, may I remind you that this is a murder investigation and not a parlour game?"

"More's the pity," Bear whispered to Tim.

"Mel, take us out of our misery, lass," Hunter said.

"Wee Gerry Littlewood. You know, the guy who worked for Thomson's Top Cars last Christmas?"

"Odious little man as I recall," Hunter said.

"But, boss, there's more."

"Just tell us, Mel. The boss is failing fast," Tim said glancing at Hunter.

"The half sausage roll that Bev Hopper kept. Well the DNA on that is from wee Gerry too."

"Fuck me, wee Gerry is Mrs Santa?" Hunter sighed. "I suppose if he dressed up like his dad does, he could be mistaken for a woman."

"An ugly woman," Rachael said.

"True. Really, I'm going to have to go, sir. All this excitement isn't good for me in my injured state and the morphine has worn off," Hunter said.

Mackay looked at Tim. "DC Myerscough, will you take DI Wilson home. No wait a minute, I don't want you on your own, Hunter."

"Don't worry, sir. I'll take him to my home. Our housekeeper, Alice, can keep an eye on him, and my sister Ailsa is coming to us for Christmas. She was DI Wilson's surgeon. I'm sure she'll have strong painkillers too."

"Your father won't be pleased," Hunter said.

"The house belongs to Ailsa and me. If he doesn't like it, he can take rooms at his club."

Hunter nodded weakly. "Thanks Tim."

The team watched as Tim and Bear lifted Hunter gently in a cradle made of their strong arms and Mel followed with his crutches.

It wasn't long before Bear and Mel bounced back into the briefing room.

"I suppose the reason wee Gerry chose to steal a car from Thomson's Top Cars is because he knows how they operate, after all, he worked there," Nadia said.

"That would make sense. Lucky we had his prints on file." Colin smiled. "Do we know what the connection is between wee Gerry and Graham Crosbie?"

"No idea," said Mackay, "but I think wee Gerry is out on bail at the moment, so we can easily find where he lives."

"I'm on it," Rachael said. "Shall Colin and I go and bring him in?"

"Yes, I'd like a DS on it. You two go," Mackay said.

"Now DC Zewedu, I don't want to wait for DC Myerscough to get back. What can you tell me about the three Santas who attacked DI Wilson?"

"From the CCTV footage there's no doubt it was Sandy Brodie, Ian Brown and Mike Bird," Bear said. "We went to Brodie's House first. He's quite a rotund chap, a real Santa type bloke. He certainly doesn't work out. He tried to shut the front door in our faces but that didn't work well for him. He's downstairs in interview room 1 waiting to tell his tale.

"We stopped by Ian Brown's place next. He lives with his sister, Marie Littlewood. We had a chat with her. Brown was furious because somebody stole all the tips the Santas made. Brodie and Bird blamed their Mrs Claus because the money went missing during her break and she was Brown's nephew, if you get me meaning."

"Yes, Bear, I'm with you so far."

"But why attack the boss?" Rachael asked. "And how did the elf end up dead?"

"We didn't find that out about the boss until we spoke to Bird, but we did get Mrs Littlewood to tell Brown to come in for an interview."

"Do you think he'll come?" Mel asked.

"Oh yes, if I were Mrs Littlewood's brother, I'd do what she said!" Bear grinned.

"It was about six o'clock by the time we got to the Bird household. An old, wiry man opened the door. His nose has been broken several times and there's are deep scars running down his left cheek."

"That's Jock Bird. He's been very quiet in recent years. I wonder what he's been up to?" Mackay mused.

"Not much, I wouldn't think. It came out he's got stage four prostate cancer. I doubt he's got much energy to raise hell now," Bear said.

"He may not raise hell, but if there's any justice that's where he's going."

"Possibly, sir. He said something similar. Anyway, he wouldn't let us in, but called Michael to the door to talk to us. As they passed in the hallway, Tim and I heard him say to the younger man. 'You're a fucking arse son, you lamped a copper and he's in a bad way.' Then Mike Bird came to speak to us."

"What does he look like?" Mackay asked.

"Maybe an inch or so shorter than his father and not quite as thin, but without the broken nose or facial scars." Bear paused and turned around because Tim had come back into the briefing room.

"He's downstairs, sir," Tim said. "Interview room 2. Apparently he doesn't want to speak to you." Tim grinned.

"That's not his choice," Mackay stood up. "Who wants to interview Bird with me?" Every detective in the room stood up. Mackay chuckled. "Come on then Zewedu, let's see what the man has to say."

PC Neil Larkin stood inside the door of interview room 2. Mackay nodded to him.

"How come I've been kept waiting so bloody long? I'm gasping for a ciggie."

"I'm terribly sorry Mr Bird. We do appreciate your time today. My colleague and I were unavoidably detained. May I offer you a cup of tea, or maybe a coffee?" Mackay asked.

"No need to be so bloody sarky. But aye, I'll take a brew, milk and three."

"Might you have time to attend to that, PC Larkin? And perhaps for us hard working coppers too." Mackay winked at Neil.

"Of course, sir. That would be my great pleasure." Neil replied with a grin.

Bear shrugged and sat down opposite Bird.

"They think they're funny – but they're no'." Bird said, trying to get Bear on his side. The big man didn't respond. Mackay sat beside Bear. He smiled at Bird, then explained that the interview would be recorded orally and visually. Bird nodded. "Just get on with it, pal. I've got a home to go to."

Neil re-entered the interview room and set three plastic containers of tea on the table and kept the fourth for himself.

"That's out a fuckin' machine. That's boggin'." Bird commented after one small sip.

"I'm sorry our beverages are not to your liking Mr Bird. Let's get the interview started and when we finish, you may be able to choose a cafeteria more to your taste." Mackay sipped his tea, as if with relish and switched on the recording. Then, after introducing everyone in the room he began to question Bird.

"For the benefit of the tape can you confirm your name and address?"

"You know fine who I am. You kent ma faither. And your boys picked me up at ma hame, ya bam. Let's get on with why I'm here."

Mackay tried another tack. "Michael Bird, you presently live with your father Jock Bird and are working for Indices in Princes Street, Edinburgh on a temporary contract as a Christmas Santa, is that correct?"

"Yes it is. Ho bloody ho."

"Sandy Brodie and Ian Brown are also employed there on a similar contract, is that so?"

"Yes. Sandy works in toys, I'm in children's clothes and Ian moves between the two so we can get breaks, have lunch and the like."

"What time did you leave work on Friday?" Bear asked.

"Five o'clock, same as always. They're strict, we have to clock in and out."

"Was anybody else with you that evening?" Mackay asked.

"Aye I gave a lift to that Graham Crosbie bastard. He's working as an elf and he's a bloody thief."

"What makes you say that?"

"Because it's true," Bird replied to Mackay and then he went on. "He nicked both jars of Santa tips. We usually split them between the three of us and it was the end of the week so there was a lot of money and both jars went missing. It had to have been him. Or that wee Gerry fucker. He may be Ian's nephew or something, but he's odd. Which man would dress up as Mrs Santa just for a temporary job? I ask you. None of us would take the jars, we'd be stealing from ourselves. I can't stand that wee punk."

"Which one?" Bear asked.

Bird thought for a minute and then said, "You're right. I can't stand either of them."

"One of my colleagues met up with you and your fellow Santas at the cash machine at the West End about six o'clock." Mackay frowned at Bird. "He heard you all arguing about money and kindly offered the three of you twenty pounds to buy yourselves a round of drinks. Can you remember how his generosity was rewarded?"

"Aye, well." Bird dropped his glance from Mackay's stare and looked at his hands that were clasped tightly below the table.

"Aye well? What the hell does that mean?" Bear shouted.

"We didn't know he was a copper, did we? I mean he didn't have a uniform or anything, did he?"

"That's true." Mackay spoke so softly and reasonably that Bear and Neil both looked at him as if he had gone mad. Then the DCI slapped the table and leaned over to shout in Bird's face. "You knew he was a human being. You knew he'd done you a kindness and you knew his money wasn't yours to take. Not suffice with stealing from the man you knocked him over on the icy pavement and left him broken and in agony."

Bird backed away as far as he could, bearing in mind that his chair was bolted to the stone floor.

Mackay looked at him in disgust. "You really are as nasty a punk as your father, aren't you? The apple didn't fall far from the tree, you despicable man."

"What, well, I mean." Bird spluttered.

"Neil, book him and lock him up."

"What's the charge?" Bird asked.

"Breathing." Mackay stood up and strode out of the room. Bear followed him and shared the most discreet high five with Neil as he left the interview room.

"Now, Sandy Brodie. You up for that, Bear, or do you want a break?"

"Lead the way, sir." The big man grinned.

Sandy Brodie sat in the interview growing increasingly impatient. How dare the coppers keep him waiting so long, with not even a cup of tea. And that lassie standing by the door looked like she was no' long out of school. The Police College at Tullyallen must be cradle snatching these days.

The room was small and dark. The only window had bars across it and was almost at the height of the ceiling. Brodie couldn't see out of it. The smell in interview rooms was nasty too. It probably didn't matter how much disinfectant the cleaners used or how much air-freshener the officers sprayed around after the room was used, no fresh air would get in here anyway. It smelled of dirt, body odour and farts. And it was clear nobody cleaned this room properly because the cobwebs hanging from the camera on the wall were so thick they could be knitted together to make a jumper. He wouldn't want to see the spider that had lived there.

He tried to push the table. Yep, bolted to the floor. Did they really think anybody would want to steal their poxy table covered in cigarette burns and carved initials?

"Mr Brodie, I'm sorry we've kept you waiting," Mackay said as he and Bear walked in.

"No you're not, you don't give a fuck. Let's just get this over with, whatever this is. It's a busy time of year and I've got places to be."

"Indeed you have, Mr Brodie. You have to be right here being interviewed about the assault and robbery to which one of my colleagues was subjected on Friday evening at the ATM at the West End of Princes Street. What would you like to tell me about that?"

"Nothing. Can I go now?"

"No," Bear said. "We're going to record this interview, Mr Brodie, orally and visually." Bear switched the tape on and introduced the four people in the room.

"Can I at least get a cuppa then? I've been here ages."

Brodie watched as Mackay nodded to the young PC and held up four fingers. She left the room quietly and then his attention returned to the detectives in front of him.

"Look, officers, it wasn't me. Mikey Bird can be a bit of a grouch and when he found out that our tips had been taken, well, he just lost the plot." Brodie tried to sound reasonable. He even attempted a smile, but neither Bear nor Mackay were in a smiling mood.

"Let's start at the beginning, shall we?" Mackay asked. "You had been working as Santa with Michael Bird and Ian Brown at Indices, Correct?"

Brodie nodded.

"For the tape, please, Mr Brodie."

"Aye. Ian's boy worked there too. Ian got him a job as an elf. No kids would get nowt for Christmas if he was a real elf. What a lazy tyke. And then I finds out bloody Mrs Santa is a man. Well, if you call wee Gerry Littlewood a man. Yea gods! What is the world coming to?"

"My thoughts exactly, Mr Brodie. What is the world coming to when a person offers to do a kindness by offering three strangers money to buy themselves a drink and gets pushed over and robbed and left badly injured for his trouble? What kind of person would do that? Because you did it, didn't you?"

"Naw, naw I didn't. It wasn't like that."

"The CCTV shows it like that," Bear said flatly. There was a sound at the door and Bear got up to open it. Only then did Brodie realise what a huge man Bear was. His shoulders were massive. He could inflict real pain. Brodie wriggled in his chair and tried to make himself look smaller. He saw Bear smiled at the PC who entered and take three of the drinks she was balancing. He handed them around and sat down again. "So, you were going to tell us how the CCTV and our colleague got it so wrong." Bear growled and Brodie cowered.

"We had to get some money because our cash had been nicked. We all wanted a drink and a chippy tea to celebrate pay day. I was driving and Ian's boy, Graham, asked for a lift. I said yes. Well you do, don't you, just to be nice?"

"But not nice enough just to say thank you to the man who offered you money for a drink."

"Look, you big black turd, I told you that wasn't me."

"And I know it was," Bear said. Brodie watched as the big man put his hands on the table.

Christ! That man's hands are bigger than my feet, he thought. He watched as Mackay caught Bear's eye. He thought he saw the boss man shake his head, then Bear leaned back in his chair. Brodie felt he had room to breathe again.

"You were saying, Mr Brodie, there were four of you in the car and you all needed to get money out of the ATM because your tips had gone missing."

"Naw, that was the thing. Young Graham said he had enough cash and he just got out the car when I parked up at Queensferry Street. He left us and walked directly into the off licence, didn't he? How come he had money when we had none? That's what I wanted to know. Thieving little bastard that he is. He took the tips jars, didn't he?"

"I don't know, did he?"

"Well he's never usually got any money. Bloody funny that he's got it the day our Santa cash goes walkabout."

"So you went to the ATM with Ian Brown and Mike Bird."

"Aye. We just walked around the corner from Queensferry Street to Princes Street had to get some cash before we could get a drink.."

"Was it a good-natured walk? Pleasant chat between you."

"Not hardly. Mikey was nipping at Ian about the tips jar and his Graham having money to go into the off-licence. And Ian's looking to me for support saying it could have been anybody. Well, it could have been wee Gerry Littlewood, bloody Mrs Santa but I didn't think it was because how would Graham have any money if he hadn't pinched our tips? It was all that made sense."

"Did you see Graham Crosbie go into the off licence?"

"Aye he wasn't there long so we saw him coming out of there and going into that big pub on the corner, I can never remember its name, but it's got all glass at the front. Saw him just as we were passing. Never offered us to buy us a pint though, did he?"

"Did that cause more friction between the three of you?"

"I suppose, aye."

"Did you see wee Gerry Littlewood in the pub?"

"Naw. We just walked past to go get our money. There aren't as many banks as there used to be. Have you noticed that? We had to walk all the way into Princes Street. It's a pain, really, having to walk so far. If we'd had our tips we could have spent them."

"And when you were at the cash machine our colleague was in front of you."

"But we didn't know he was a pig, did we? We were just standing in line."

"That's not the way we heard it," Bear said. "We heard the three of you were arguing about who should buy your drinks because your tips had been stolen. Is that the way it was?"

"Aye. A bit of a barnie." Brodie nodded.

"That's why my colleague offered you some money to get yourselves a beer. It was kind of him." Mackay stared at Brodie. "But what thanks did he get?"

"When he opened his wallet there was a real wad of cash in it. I couldn't believe it. And he only gave us a twenty."

"But it was his wad of cash and his twenty that he didn't have to give away at all!" Bear stood up and shouted.

Brodie was relieved when he saw Mackay wave his hand to indicate that Bear should sit down again. That man was built like a tree.

"It was you that made a grab for the wallet, wasn't it?"

"Aye, but I didn't push him. That was Mikey. And when Ian saw his ID in his wallet, he told us to run. We didn't know he was hurt."

"But you knew he'd slipped, and you just left him there on the pavement in agony. He was calling for help, but you just left him." Bear grimaced.

"He's a copper. We didn't want any trouble."

"Well, you've got more trouble than you can bloody imagine," the big man said.

"I think we've heard enough, Bear. Book him and charge him and stick him in the cells for tonight. Then you can get yourself something to eat."

"Thanks sir, that all sounds good."

"So I'll be here overnight?"

"Yes. Haven't you brought your pyjamas?" Bear muttered scornfully.

Ian Brown didn't know Brodie had been interviewed a few minutes before him. But he smelled *Lynx Africa* aftershave and guessed Brodie had been in this room. How many blokes wore that much perfume you could smell them after they left? Mind you it had to be an improvement. This room had no air in it, and it was musty as hell. He tried to pull his chair back from the table a bit because it was tight against his belly, but it was firmly held in place. He might have guessed.

There was a cop standing by the door. He didn't look any older than Graham. Ian felt he must be getting older. Then he smiled, there was no other way to go, was there? The youngster didn't smile. The door opened, a tall blond guy, who was built like a brick shit house held the door for a dainty little Asian woman. Ian always had trouble telling the Chinese from the Japanese and he had no chance with Korean, Indonesians and the like. A week's holiday in Bali hadn't helped with that either.

The woman sat opposite him, and the big fellow took the chair beside her. Ian wasn't sure the furniture would cope with the strain, but decided it wasn't his risk to worry about. The blond man cleared his throat and Ian looked up at his face. He noticed the man's brilliant blue eyes. Ian had never seen such vividly coloured eyes before and even with his broken nose, there was no getting away from the fact he was handsome. Ian mused that he might even turn for him. He smiled at the thought.

"Is assault and robbery of a police detective amusing to you, Ian?" The woman asked.

Ian shook his head and straightened his face.

Then, without any introduction the woman switched on a recording device beside her and informed him that he was being interviewed under caution. The interview was to be recorded and she gave the names of all the people in the room. It seemed her name was Chan, he didn't catch the name of the young man by the door, and he had no chance of pronouncing the blond fellow's name. She referred to him as Tim. That would do.

The man asked him about Friday evening, and he had to admit that it was strange Graham hadn't needed to go to the bank. He agreed that the Santas tips jars had gone missing but told them he was sure Graham wouldn't have taken them.

"How can you be sure?" DC Chan asked him.

"I can't be sure, but he's my nephew, my sister's boy and I know him."

"Of course, you know him and love him don't you?" Nadia asked.

"I wouldn't go that far, he's my nephew, but I'd count my change if he went shopping for me."

"So he might have taken the tips?"

"Maybe, but he's scared shitless of Mike Bird."

"So who do you think took is more likely to have taken the money?"

"Probably the wee shite Gerry Littlewood."

"Why do you say that?" she asked.

"I've done business with his father in the past and always had to count my fingers afterwards."

"Could Gerry and Graham have shared the money?"

"Doubt it. They didn't have much to do with each other and Gerry wasn't exactly the sharing kind. Did he kill our lad? I bet he did! Vicious little bastard. Did he?"

"Why do you say that?"

"Graham had started going out with a lassie, Rosie her name is, worked on the perfume counter at Indices. He couldn't stop talking about her."

"What's that got to do with Gerry killing Graham?"

"Gerry made a play for her, didn't he? All dressed up as Mrs Santa. Well, she laughed in his face and next thing you know, she and Graham are an item."

"A bit much to go from not getting the girl to killing the elf," Tim said.

"Maybe. But I'd lay money on Gerry being up to no good any day of the week."

Then the detectives questioned Ian about the events of Friday evening with him. Although he claimed vehemently he'd had nothing to do with the attack on the copper, and the other two Santas were the guilty parties, the police officers listened, but he didn't think they looked convinced. It was no surprise when they charged him, and he ended up in the cell in between Brodie and Bird.

. . .

Colin and Rachael had picked Gerry up at his home. He acted as if he had nothing better to do at this time of year than be interviewed by the boys, or girls, in blue.

The Christmas trees in peoples' windows all decorated in coloured lights reminded him of how happy this time of year was meant to be. As they drove over The Mound, Gerry could see the Christmas rides turning and the big wheel rising slowly to his right. There were so many bright lights. Beautiful. He glanced over at the Christmas tree all decked in shining white lights. Every year Norway gifted a beautiful Christmas tree to Edinburgh in thanks for the assistance Scottish troops gave that country during the second World War. That was nice and it was all so pretty. Gerry sighed. He wasn't sure the hours ahead of him were going to be so pleasant.

When they got to the station, Gerry asked Colin if he could nip into the little boys room before they started their interview. Colin nodded and he and Rachael waited outside for him. The interview room was hot and stuffy. It was obvious to Gerry it had been in use not long before.

They all sat down, and Rachael explained the procedure for recording the interview. Apparently the uniform at the door was Neil Larkin. Gerry thought about where he knew that name from. Probably the last time he got nicked.

Colin began the interview. "I understand you were working at Indices as Mrs Claus," he said.

"Yep."

"An interesting choice," Rachael said.

"I'm on bail and there aren't too many places that'd give me a chance. All the jobs for Santas and Elves were taken, so I said I'd do Mrs Claus. I'm not bad at it, if I say so myself."

"Did you steal the Santas tips jars?"

"What; steal from the Bird clan, do you think I've got a death wish?"

"Somebody took it." Rachael stated flatly.

"Maybe so, but it wasn't me."

"Do you know who it was?"

"Not for certain, no."

"What does that mean?" Colin asked.

"It means I think that back-stabbing little shit Graham Crosbie probably took the money, but I can't prove it."

"You didn't like Graham?"

"Gosh, you're quick for a copper, aren't you? No I didn't like him, and I'm glad he's dead, but I didn't kill him."

"Who said anything about killing him?"

"No, it's just funny that..."

"Is Graham being murdered funny, Gerry?" Rachael asked. "Why did you steal a car from Thomson's? Was it so you could make a quick getaway after you'd killed Graham Crosbie?"

"Tell me about Friday evening, Gerry," Colin asked.

"All of it?"

"Yes, from the time you left work."

"The shop shuts at five, so I was out of there pretty quick."

"Because you'd taken the tips jars and didn't want anybody to see you?" Rachael asked.

"Because I was tired and wanted a drink. I was thirsty. I didn't steal the tips jars, okay?"

"Let's assume you didn't take the tips jars," Colin said. "What happened?"

"The Santas and fucking Graham Crosbie took a car along to the West End."

"It's a short journey to take a car." Colin observed.

"Aye, but it stops you getting locked in the staff carpark overnight. If your car's there too long they lock the gates. Security do it just for fun. They're bastards."

Colin nodded.

"They didn't even offer me a lift, did they? So I just runs along to *Greggs*, the bakers like, I gets a couple o' sausage rolls to have with my pint and stops into Ryan's. It's the closest decent pub."

"What happened then?"

"Look, lass, all I'm doing is sitting quietly having my drink and munching on my chow and playing *Candy Crush* on my phone."

"Candy Crush? Very butch," Rachael said.

"Piss off. You asked me to tell you."

"Go on, Gerry."

"Aye, well tell her no' to be judgey. I wasn't doing no harm. Then fucking' Graham comes in. He's too wee to sit on the bar stools comfortably, so he gets his pint and looks around. He clocks me, doesn't he? And he starts givin' it laldy. He's bellowin' at the staff, touchin' up the lassies and getting told to fuck off left right and centre."

Colin nodded. "So you'd got to the pub before Graham did although you didn't get a lift?"

"Yep. Like I said, I ran along. And I think he must have stopped in at Oddbins because he had a bag full of drink with him. Then, he's shoutin' the odds, but it's me that gets turfed out, just for eating my sausage rolls. I'd a half a one left and they just took it off me. Have you ever heard the like?"

He sounded so indignant; Rachael had to smile.

"Well seein' it wasn't your grub lass."

"I suppose so." Rachael agreed.

"Then I'm just on my way home and I gets a text from Graham saying Rosie and him have a good laugh about my willy and how it's the size of a peanut *M&M* and I never did it for her, but he always hits the spot and if I wants to see what a real man looks like he'll be up at the Castle Terrace carpark tonight. Well! What would you do?"

"I'd consider the source and get the bus home," Colin said.

"Aye, well no' me."

"I certainly wouldn't steal a car after I'd been drinking and murder the guy who made such silly remarks," Rachael said.

"But you're no' a man, lass."

"Well spotted."

"And I didn't kill him."

"Okay, so what did you do? You must have got the bus out to Thomson's Top Cars, so you planned to nick a car. Why there? There must have been somewhere more convenient, and I thought you liked Jamie and Frankie," Colin said.

"They're no' the worst. But I knew they'd be closing and bringing the cars into the showroom. I figured it would be an easy pick. I gets the car, it was smart. I might get one like that."

"I wouldn't count on it for a while," Rachael said.

"Anyway, there's the wee bastard up on the first storey. I hear laughing and a voice saying. 'Rosie, oh Rosie, you need this lovely big cock and you'll no' regret it."

"Was Rosie there?"

"Was she fuck, lass. He's on the ground and looks drunk out of his skull. I gets out the car, and shouts at him."

"I hear a voice, saying, 'what you doin' here, wee Gerry?' but it's not Graham's voice."

"I said I'd got his text and come like he said, to have it out with him. Then I heard a noise behind me, I turned round, and I get whacked over the head with a great big spanner that was in the car. And that's me on the deck. I know nothing else, but I know who hit me."

"Well, who would have thought it?" Mackay said as he called the morning briefing to order. "Well done, Colin and Rachael. Good to see you feel well enough to be here, Hunter."

"Congrats, the drinks are on you tonight!" Bear shouted.

"Thanks, sir. It's an exciting finish in the run up to Christmas," Rachael said.

"Shut up, Bear we're going to my mother's," Mel said. There was a jeer went round the room with cries of 'best behaviour, Bear', 'Don't upset the mother.' And 'it'll be a cheap round tonight then'.

Mackay smacked his folder on the desk. "Shut up you lot. Colin, and Rachael got to the bottom of all this, tell us what happened."

"Let them have their fun, sir. They deserve it. Good Lord, working that hard on the run up to Christmas can't have been a barrel of laughs," Hunter Wilson said. He winced as he moved his leg on to the top of an upturned wastepaper basket to support it in a raised position.

"Don't worry, boss. I can wait." Colin smiled at Hunter and stood up to applause from the team. He bowed in an exaggerated fashion towards his colleagues. "It was a lot simpler than we thought.

"There's no doubt that all three of the Santas from Indices were involved in the assault on the boss," Colin turned to Hunter. "Brodie made a snatch at your wallet which caused you to fall on the slippery pavement." He nodded towards Hunter. "Brown knocked you over with his fat belly and Bird noticed your ID and warned them all to run."

"We got that much from the CCTV," Nadia added. "Of course the fact they all blamed each other and didn't argue that those on the film were them confirmed their involvement."

"I don't suppose they'll get that long, but at least we caught them," Hunter said.

"You might be surprised, Hunter," Mackay said. "Assaulting a police officer, serious bodily harm, robbery with violence, obstructing the course of justice..." I'm going to ask the Procurator Fiscal to throw the book at them. How are you now anyway?"

"Still sore and on strong painkillers. Also, I can't believe how weird it feels to use my other hand to pee."

"Too much information, boss," Tim laughed. "What about the murder, how did we get that so wrong, Rache?"

"It was true there was bad blood between Gerry and Graham, *Loves' Labours Lost* and all that, but what we overlooked was that Graham was living with his mother and his uncle and he and his uncle had fallen out big time about the tips jar. Graham was dead before wee Gerry even got to Castle Terrace carpark."

"Aha!" Mackay exclaimed.

"Ian can't stand wee Gerry and he thought Graham had stolen the tips jars and that had caused him a lot of grief with Mike Bird. Ian was scared of Bird.

"Most sensible folk are scared of the Bird clan. They're evil," MacKay said.

"But he thought of a way to implicate Gerry and to try to get the money back from Graham. But it all went sour.

"Ian texted Graham and told him to come to the Castle Terrace carpark to talk about how to sort it with Bird. Ian knew Graham would be three sheets to the wind and wouldn't think it through."

"And Graham agreed?" Tim asked.

"Well, he said he'd be there." Rachael shrugged.

"So how did wee Gerry get involved?" Mel asked.

"When Graham arrived at the carpark, Ian got him to text wee Gerry to challenge him to a cock fight, supposedly for a laugh but that must have diverted Graham's attention. Literally. It was to be a mine's bigger than yours contest according to wee Gerry," Colin said.

"I bet it's not!" Bear joked.

"Ah, but I'm the one with two kids." Colin teased.

"Go on," Mackay said.

"While Graham was texting Gerry, Ian punched him and knocked him out. Gerry arrived in the stolen car. He admits to the theft, by the way, and as he's on bail, I doubt that'll go well for him." Rachael looked at Hunter.

"It might go better if he'll give evidence for us," Hunter said.

"Agreed," Mackay smiled. "So what happened next?"

"Ian crept up behind Gerry and must have seen the tools that Jamie left in the car he stole. Gerry was given a right good whack with the large spanner and, as Ian was wearing gloves, his prints weren't on the implement."

"Ian just hadn't reckoned on Gerry seeing him." Nadia nodded.

"Putting the rest together exactly is more difficult, until Ian confesses, but he will. He's a bully and all bullies are cowards. It's clear Grahm was hit with the same spanner too. He must have been hit much harder than Gerry and it was his blood and DNA that we found on it first, but after Gerry's story the lab looked again, and there were traces of his DNA too," Colin said. "It was a pity Gerry's DNA was missed the first time, but the lump on his head proved he was telling the truth."

"Why didn't he get it seen to?" Hunter asked.

"Because he was on bail and not meant to be stealing cars or getting involved in fights." Colin answered.

"Of course, sorry." Hunter muttered.

"It's also why we couldn't find the booze Graham bought at Oddbins." Rachael added. "Ian was too stupid and too greedy to leave it in the carpark. When Gerry came round he saw Ian taking it home. When the CSIs examine his place they'll no doubt find the bag with all the drink in it, and the two tips jars that Graham stole covered in Graham's DNA and fingerprints, probably under the bed, or someplace stupid like that."

"Poor sod." Mackay said.

"Who?" Hunter asked.

"Graham. I just hope the few quid he got was worth it."

Jessica arrived at Tim's door, she was excited to be invited to his Christmas Eve party and dressed to the nines for it. Tim answered the door and greeted her warmly, kissing her gently on the cheek.

"Come in, come in. What can I get you to drink?"

She took her coat off in the hall and handed it to Tim. She suddenly felt quite shy. "Would a gin and tonic be okay?" She asked as she followed him up the stairs.

Tim opened the door to a large, dining room that had been decorated in red and white. Holly decorated the tables and mistletoe was hanging in large bunches from the ceiling. "Let me introduce you to everyone, Jess," he said as he led her around the room and made sure she met his father, Sir Peter, his sister Ailsa whom she knew from the hospital and Ailsa's boyfriend Simon. Jess also knew Bear from the hospital and met his girlfriend Mel and lastly, her former patient, Hunter Wilson was sitting on a comfortable chair with his injured leg supported by an ancient looking pouffe. By looking around the room, Jessica guessed it was probably an antique.

"What are you drinking?" Bear asked.

"Gin and tonic, please." Jessica walked over to him and whispered in his ear. "This isn't really a regular thing is it?"

"Whatever do you mean?"

"Tim told me he threw a Christmas Eve party every year and wanted me to join it this year."

Bear laughed. "You've got him bang to rights," he said softly. "Tim's never had a Christmas Eve party in his life and probably won't again, but he put this together because he wants to get to know you better. Don't be too hard on him, he's one of the good guys." Then in a loud voice Bear said, "Is that enough ice, Jess?" He handed her drink to her and went on, "And don't miss the lemon drizzle cake, it's delicious."

THE BRUNTSFIELD BOOK GROUP

"I don't want to go. I don't have to go. I don't need a reason. I just don't want to go." Jane was becoming irritated by Rachael's repeated attempts to persuade her to come to the Bruntsfield Book Group's annual outing which, this year, was to a lodge in the highlands of Scotland.

"Please Janey, you never come. And I'm always there on my own, little miss no mates. Everyone else brings their partners."

"Well don't go."

"I want to go, and I want you to come with me."

"What is it your mum says? I want doesn't get."

"Janey I'm not five. Please come. Just this once and if you don't like it, I promise I'll never ask you again."

"I won't know anybody."

"You know Lydia and Simon."

"Great, the only couple I know, I don't like."

"You've met Howard and his wife."

"He's a hundred and three and all his wife talks about is knitting."

"He's seventy-five and Cynthia has many hobbies and interests."

"None that I share."

"You liked Theo and Ryan when you met them."

"I met them once in a rainstorm, sheltering outside the library. I have nothing in common with them. All they talked about is the authors they know, most of whom I'd never heard of and their niece, whom I've never met and am never likely to. Who else is going?"

"Paula and Sean."

"I don't know them."

"No, but they're nice. You'll like them. And Sylvia and Bert."

"I don't know them either. Rache..."

"Please Janey. Come this once and if you don't like it, you never have to come again."

"I don't have to come this time." Jane sighed. "Don't give me that look."

"What look?" Rachael tried to look innocent. "How about I open a bottle of wine and we can talk about it some more and you can have a good think? That would be a good idea, wouldn't it?"

Two bottles of Pinot Grigio and later, a long relaxing bath with Rachael, made Jane feel as good as she had for a while. Rachael offered herself and Jane teased her until Rachael begged for mercy. None was forthcoming. Then the women fell into bed. Jane pleasured and played with her wife until Rachael's come ran into her hand.

"You are amazing, Sergeant Renwick." Rachael smiled up at her.

"You're not so bad yourself, DC Anderson."

"Not bad? I'm fab-u-lous, and I'll prove it."

Rachael disappeared beneath the covers and caressed Jane's breasts, tickling her nipples with her tongue. She kissed her way gently down Jane's body and was rewarded with groans of pleasure.

Before she knew Jane's ultimate satisfaction had been achieved she popped her head back out and smiled at Jane.

"Have you had enough now?"

"Bitch! You can't leave me like this."

"You can't leave me alone in the lodge at the book group social."

"Fuck me Rachael. I'll fucking come but I can't stand this."

"You'll come; I heard you say you'll come. Damn right you'll come."

It was sometime later when Jane had been fully satisfied, Rachael started to fondle her wife again.

"No, no more Rache. I can't cope. You've had me, darling. I'm yours." Jane rolled towards Rachael and they both smiled. "You're a bitch you know that. Threatening to leave me aching unless I agreed to go to that bloody lodge in the highlands for a long weekend with you and your boring book group."

"Don't tell anyone, they all think I'm the nice one. Still, I'm glad you're going to be with me. And the group is not as boring as you'd think. Half of them don't like each other and the rest hate the others."

"Then why do you all go away together?"

"It's Edinburgh. Nobody is meant to know we dislike each other."

It was raining heavily as they drove out of Edinburgh and headed towards the A9 for the long drive North to the lodge. As they drove over the Queensferry Crossing above the River Forth, Rachael began to explain the intricacies of the book group dynamics to Jane.

"I'm the newbie. The group was set up about fifteen years ago by Howard and Cynthia after he retired, and she'd had her stroke."

"Great."

"No, don't be like that. She's recovered well. But because they're a couple that's why all the other partners go on the outing. This year our themed colour is red."

"Hmm, so that's why I had to wear red socks. Why is there a themed colour?"

"I don't know. I never asked. You can ask Howard."

"Not likely. I don't care that much." Jane frowned. "This rain is heavy. I don't like to think what it'll be like up north. It'll be snowy and could be deep." She glanced at Rachael. "Anyway, tell me the rest. Where do Lydia and Simon fit in?"

"They're both retired too." Rachael heard Jane sigh. She ignored it. "They live next door to Howard and Cynthia. Only Lydia comes to the group. Simon and Howard can't stand each other. They're always making snidey, sarcastic remarks when they meet. That can be funny, but most of the time it's a bit wearing."

"I can see Howard's point. Simon is an arse. I can't imagine what it was like working in the council when he was Lord Provost. Oh why did I say I'd come to this? It's a weekend of my life I'll never get back. Look! That rain is turning to sleet. I told you it would."

"Stop moaning, Janey. You're coming because you love me and because I bribed you into it."

"You did! You little shit." Jane grinned at Rachael and told her to carry on with her explanation of the dynamics of the group.

"Theo and Ryan are a nice couple. Of course I don't know Ryan so well, because he works for a lawyer in Glasgow and is never back in time for the book group. Theo works in as a barista at Café Nero since his breakdown. Before that he was a lawyer with the council. He worked with Simon then."

"That's probably why he had a breakdown. Are there any normal people in the group?"

"I'm not going to fuck you, you're driving, and it might be dangerous, especially when we get onto the single-track roads."

"Shut up. Single track roads in the snow. That's all I bloody need."

"I'll drive if you want. Just stop complaining."

"No, you won't." Jane sighed. "Who are the others?"

"Paula and Sean. Only Paula comes to the book group. She's a retired teacher. But Sean always reads the books, so we get his opinion whether we want it or not."

"What a control freak."

"Don't think it's meant that way. It's just he was chief librarian back in the day, I think. He had problems with Simon and the council then."

"Surprise, surprise."

"Yeh. That's why he doesn't come. And Sylvia and Bert both come. They're retired, but he was a lay preacher, so he always talks about their time working as missionaries in Uganda and finds a religious angle to whatever we read. It can be funny if it's a crime thriller. Sylvia is lovely. She was a nurse, but her concentration... She rarely finishes a book now."

"Please save me!" Jane exclaimed. "This sounds even worse than I thought. Do we really have to go, Rache?"

"Yes, I said we're coming. And we've bought all that food. It'll be fun." Rachael squinted through the windscreen. "Can the wipers go any faster."

"If they go any faster they'll turn into helicopter blades!"

Rachael grinned at Jane. "We're cooking with Theo and Ryan tonight. You said you like them. Of course, we play games, go for walks and the book for this weekend is an Alexander McCall-Smith, so it's not too long."

"Cook? Games? Read? Bloody hell, Rache. You never told me any of this. On top of all that this weather is getting worse. It'll be even deeper snow the further north we go. This is crazy. Can't we turn around?"

"Shut up. You know we can't. We'd look like real wimps if we said we couldn't get there and everybody else did. Anyway, the highlands are beautiful in the snow. I brought Scrabble."

"Whoopy-do."

"Janey, you'll have fun. I've got a couple of chickens as the main course for our meal. Theo and I decided we're doing a roast chicken dinner. It's not difficult. Theo and Ryan are putting together a fruit salad, and we'll finish with cheese and biscuits."

"You mean I've got to share that lovely brie we bought. Damn." Jane smiled. She'd have to make the most of this, although the whole weekend sounded ghastly to her. "Let's stop for lunch the next place we see."

They pulled over at a little café just outside of Aviemore. They chose a table by a window, and, despite the falling snow, they couldn't help admiring the views.

"You can see why the skiing is so good up here. We should get a group together and take an Air B&B for a weekend and come skiing," Jane said.

"That would be fun. I remember when we were little, we used to come north at the beginning of the school holidays every summer. Mum used to make a picnic and we'd stop around Drumochter Summit. Dad would insist that some of the sandwiches were lamb."

"Why?"

"It was his annual joke, to feed lamb sandwiches to the sheep."

"Oh no! That's so bad,"

"It made us laugh."

"Yuck." They finished their meal and took a few extra minutes to have a cup of tea. "There's no chamomile." Jane frowned.

"Don't grumble, Janey. Anyway, shall we motor on?" Rachael stood up. "The journey could take a bit longer than we anticipated in this weather."

"Good!"

The waitress came over and they paid their bill in cash.

"Where is this lodge anyway?"

"It's on a farm southeast of Thurso. I'll get the directions out."

"Is it on a B road?"

"The lodge is on a track across farmland."

"You get the directions and make sure we don't get lost in the middle of nowhere. We have nothing to drink but gin and white wine."

"And we'd have to eat the brie."

"On second thoughts, don't worry about getting us lost."

. . .

When Jane and Rachael arrived at the lodge, Lydia and Simon were already there wearing bright red jumpers. They had taken occupation of the largest bedroom on the ground floor. It had a double aspect and a sitting area as well as a king-sized bed. The greeting between the two couples was courteous rather than warm. Jane tried to smile but her efforts came out more as a grimace.

Theo and Ryan arrived immediately after the women and eased the tension a bit. They greeted the others with hugs and seemed happier to be there than Jane could credit. They both wore red hats and Ryan had a red ruck sack too.

"I'm sure Howard and Cynthia will want the other ground floor room, so shall we take our bags upstairs and scout out what's there?" Rachael suggested.

"Let's do that," Theo agreed. "Then we can start to fill the fridge. I hope it's already got ice in it."

"It does," Simon said. "It's the first thing I checked."

After checking out the best room, Jane thought.

"Come on, Janey, grab a bag." Rachael said as she picked up her holdall and followed Theo up the stairs.

Jane was staring at her phone. "No phone signal," she said as she returned her phone to her pocket.

"Nope, no Wi-Fi either," Ryan said.

"And I doubt you'll find CCTV for miles." Rachael laughed. "Come on, Janey. Shake a leg."

Jane was pleasantly surprised that all the rooms were en-suite and the four bedrooms on the first floor were very similar, so there was hardly any discussion about who took which room. Jane and Rachael took the room next to Theo and Ryan leaving the bedrooms on the other side of the hall for Sylvia and Bert, Paula, and Sean.

It wasn't long before everyone else had arrived and got themselves settled. They all took their contributions down to the kitchen. Jane thought they might have to stay for a week to make a dent in the quantity of food they'd all brought but immediately dismissed this as unbearable.

"I'm going to go for a run after that long drive," she said. "Would anybody like to come with me?"

"But there's snow on the ground," Sylvia said.

"It's not too deep on the path." Ryan looked out of the window. "I'll come for a run with you, Jane." He pulled his red hat out of his pocket and smiled.

"I might go for a walk instead," Rachael said. "I just don't run fast enough to keep up with you, even when there's no snow, Jane."

Everybody except Howard, Cynthia and Lydia chose to go for a walk too.

"We'll have some tea and biscuits ready for when you get back," Cynthia said.

Jane went upstairs to get her running shoes and Rachael took her walking boots out of the car then she watched Jane take off at her usual pace, with Ryan matching her step for step.

It was a bit like herding cats to get the others organised to go for their walk, but eventually Rachael agreed with Theo that she would walk at the front of the group, and he would be her back man to make sure nobody got left behind.

It came as no surprise to Rachael that Simon wanted to walk at the front too. She thought asking his opinion on the book they were reading over the weekend would be a safe topic, but immediately regretted it. He not only told her what he thought of that, but also gave her a potted history of the author since he moved to Scotland from his birthplace in Southern Zimbabwe, his time as a professor of Law at the University of Edinburgh and was just about to start on about the author's wife's medical career when Rachael saw Jane and Theo running back towards them. She had never been so pleased to see anybody.

"Simon, I can see the runners," she said. "Shall we wait for the other walkers and then start our journey back? That way we'll get back at a similar time for our tea."

Rachael made a point of walking back with Sean and Paula. Nobody could miss them in their bright red home knitted scarves. Paula's jolly stories about things her pupils had said or misunderstood were much more fun to listen to than Simon's monologue had been.

Rachael mentioned this to Sean and Paula. Paula pursed her lips. Sean frowned.

"That man is evil," he said. "I don't know how Lydia puts up with him. I certainly couldn't. And he was even worse when I was trying to get money out of him for the libraries when he was at the council. Give a man a little power..."

"You shouldn't burden Rachael that way, Sean," Paula said.

"Perhaps, dear. I'm sorry Rachael. But you didn't have to put up with him. Libraries benefit the poorest folk the most, but they didn't vote for his party. He was never a deep thinker, I suppose." Sean looked at the ground and then at his wife before he changed tone and subject to the days when he was a librarian. He had some funny stories about unusual books he had seen requested by library members. Some of which they wanted wrapped in paper bags so that people couldn't see what they had borrowed. All three of them were laughing as they took their muddy boots off in the entrance porch of the lodge.

"Cynthia has made tea, Lydia put together homemade lemonade and I put the biscuits on a plate. Help yourselves." Howard smiled. "Have we all finished the book already, or shall we discuss it tomorrow?"

"You really are a bloody fool, man. Of course we're not going to talk about the book today."

Rachael looked at Howard and saw he looked hurt.

"No need to be nasty, Simon," Paula said. "But tomorrow would probably be better." She smiled at Howard.

Lydia handed Simon a glass of the lemonade, and then gave some to Rachael, Ryan, and Bert. Everybody else poured themselves a cup of tea and the group went to sit in the living room.

"I think it's our young people making dinner tonight. What are we having Rachael?" Lydia asked.

Rachael watched Simon sip his drink and sit down before she said, "I brought two chickens. I thought we could make a roast chicken dinner."

"Ooh that sounds delicious," Cynthia said.

"Ryan and I brought all sorts of fresh fruit for a fruit salad and a tub of Luca's ice cream so we could have that with it," Theo said.

"I love Luca's ice cream. It's the best. But how did you manage to get ice cream here?" Howard asked.

Theo laughed. "By the magic of a cool box. They are wonderful things."

"And a swift transfer to the freezer when we got here." Ryan added. "And we all brought some delicious cheeses for afterwards."

"If we can prize the brie out of Jane's hands. Then we can all have some." Rachael added with a smile. "Shall we start our preparations? Then we could eat at seven?"

"Perfect!" Lydia smiled.

"My goodness, you took your walk at the right time. Look at the snow!" Bert said.

"Oh it's getting heavier. I'm glad we're all safe and warm in here for the night," Cynthia said.

"We certainly couldn't try to go anywhere in that." Sean agreed. "Even with our four-wheel drive I wouldn't want to risk it. Is there any more tea in the pot?"

With that said and the time of the meal agreed, Jane and Rachael went through to the kitchen. They set the oven to pre-heat and started preparing potatoes and vegetables for a traditional meal that they thought everyone in the group would enjoy.

Theo and Ryan took the cheeses out of the fridge to breathe before starting to prepare the fruit salad.

The other members of the group divided themselves into groups. Simon, Cynthia, and Sylvia took the opportunity to rest in their rooms while Howard, Lydia, Bert, and Paula played a few hands of bridge. Then Lydia and Bert mentioned they still had to finish the book, so the game broke up and they went to get their copies of the novel.

"I have a book club copy. It has suggested questions and points for discussion at the back. I'll get it to show you." Howard said to Paula. He went into his room to get it.

Rachael and Jane enjoyed cooking together. They had fun chatting with Ryan and Theo too. Jane opened a bottle of Pinot Grigio to share with the men while they prepared the meal.

"Cooks' perks," she said.

It was six o'clock and Ryan had set the large table in the dining room. The chicken and vegetables were cooking, so Theo suggested they put out a few bowls of olives, nuts and crisps and tell everyone to gather in the living room for pre-dinner drinks.

"Good idea, you do that, Theo. Could you find a bowl or something to put some ice in, Ryan? I'll go and knock on bedroom doors and tell those who are resting what we're doing," said Rachael.

"Okay, honey." Jane smiled. "Perhaps this weekend won't be so bad after all."

Rachael came back downstairs and accepted the bottle of Peroni Jane had opened for her. "Everyone awake?"

"Yes. Sylvia's on her way, she's just putting on a fresh blouse before coming downstairs but it took me ages to get a reply from Howard and Cynthia's room. I think they were fast asleep. Anyway, they'll just be a minute, they're getting changed for dinner."

"Howard said he was going to get a book to show me but never came back. I don't doubt he's been sleeping," Paula said.

"Changing for dinner is a good idea, I'm going to put on a fresh shirt. What about you, Theo?" Ryan smiled.

"Yes, I'm up for that. We won't be long, Rachael, just start without us."

"We intend to!" Rachael smiled. "I got nothing from Simon."

Rachael turned to Lydia and sipped her beer. "But I know he doesn't say anything if he thinks nothing needs to be said. Oh, you've changed your jumper too. That blue one suits your colouring so much better."

"Thank you. It's a favourite. No Simon often doesn't speak if he doesn't need to but talks endlessly on other occasions. It can be most off putting sometimes. He'll be with us shortly, I'm sure. He's probably having a sleep like the others after your nice walk earlier but won't want to admit to being tired. I'll pour him a whisky. He'll smell it! I saw some Ardbeg, is it in the kitchen?" Lydia said.

"Yes, it is. Help yourself," Bert said as Lydia moved swiftly into the kitchen.

She came back out again almost immediately. Silly me, I forgot to take a glass for Simon's drink, and did somebody say there's clementine tonic? I'd love some to go with this Seville gin."

"I'll get it for you, dear," Paula said. "I put a box of it in the fridge. There's elderflower too. I like that for a change every now and then."

There were various conversations floating about the living room. Jane quite surprised herself by how much she enjoyed the chat. It seemed she even had something in common with Cynthia who had been a keen runner in her day.

"You ran the first London marathon?" Jane confirmed.

"Yes. And I've run Amsterdam, Boston, and Sydney too. Have you run any marathons, Jane?"

"No. I've never even thought about it."

"Oh you should. There's a great sense of achievement finishing one, especially with a personal best time."

When Theo and Ryan returned to the group, Theo whispered to Rachael. She nodded and called everybody to take their seats as dinner was ready.

They came out from the kitchen. Rachael carried a tray with bowls of vegetables and potatoes, Theo carried the platters with the chickens.

"Everything's ready and Theo has sliced and jointed the chickens, so let's eat and enjoy," she said.

Lydia looked around. "Simon isn't here yet. It's not like him to miss a whisky. I'll go and get him; you all sit down. We won't be a minute."

With a general chatter and shuffling of chairs the group moved across to the table and chose where to sit. They all agreed the meal smelt delicious and began to help themselves from the dishes on the table. As wine was passed around, the conversation grew louder.

Then stopped.

Lydia screamed.

Jane looked at Rachael and the two women raced towards the sound. Paula and Theo were just ahead of them.

"He's dead!" Lydia cried.

"Goodness no, dear. He's probably just exhausted after the fresh air and exercise," Paula said. Then she looked more closely at Simon. She turned away and threw up all over the rug. "His head. It's nearly off." She choked.

"Don't be silly, do you know how hard it is to cut a head off?" Theo asked. "I've just jointed the chickens and that was difficult enough. He's probably cut himself shaving." He looked at Simon, then caught Jane's eye. "He never did this shaving," he said. The man turned pale and looked like he was going to pass out.

Jane and Rachael moved to see Simon more closely. There was a deep cut across his throat from one carotid artery to the other. He could never have inflicted an injury like that on himself, nor had he stood a chance of survival.

This was murder.

"I need everybody except Rachael out of this room. I'm treating this as a crime scene."

"Crime scene? That's a bit melodramatic," Theo said.

Jane glowered at him.

Lydia was shivering. Jane was not surprised; it was a natural reaction to the shock of seeing her husband lying dead on the bed. Jane glanced at Rachael. She nodded imperceptibly towards Lydia. Rachael took the hint.

"Paula, would you be kind enough to take Lydia through to the dining room. I think she needs to sit down and have a strong drink. She's in a terrible state." Rachael said softly.

"Theo, could you ask everyone else to stay out of here just now. We don't want anybody else coming into this room, it will just upset them.

"And it *is* a crime scene. I'll call the police," Jane said. She pulled out her phone. "Fuck! No signal." She tried to send a message to DI Regina Jowell who was her boss at the Major Incident Team in Gartcosh to report the crime. No Wi-Fi. "Fuck." She muttered. "Rachael, have you got signal?"

"Not likely, but I'll check." Rachael looked at her phone. "No pet."

"Is there a landline here?"

"I don't think so. I didn't notice one, but I'll have a look. I'll see if anybody else has signal."

"Thank you. This is a bloody mess."

"Literally."

The group were sitting around the dining room table looking shocked. "With no landline, no mobile phone signal, no Wi-Fi and snow on the ground, we're on our own," Jane said.

"What do you mean, dear?" Cynthia asked.

"She means we can't help Simon right now, so we might as well eat dinner," Howard said.

"Yes, I'm hungry. Pass the potatoes before they're stone cold, Howard," Sean said.

"How can you think of food?" Paula asked. She sipped a strong gin and tonic. Holding the glass with two hands.

"They haven't seen him," Theo said. "Oh God, it was awful. I'll never shave again."

Jane looked around the group. "That's not what I mean at all. Eat if you like, but we have a murderer amongst us, and I, for one, plan to find out who killed Simon."

"Don't be silly, Jane. None of us could kill anybody," Ryan argued.

"Then how do you suggest the man in the room next door had his neck sliced from ear to ear?" Jane looked serious. "Nobody but us has been in the lodge, have they?"

"No." He agreed. "That's true."

"Then one of us is a murderer, and I'd like to know who. Wouldn't you?"

Jane stared around the table. Nobody met her eye. Then she noticed that she had picked up a joint of chicken and was nibbling it. She was hungry too.

"Does anyone have a notebook I can use?"

Everyone stood up. Nervous laughter filled the air.

"Rache, could you get me your notebook and a pen. Then let's go through everything we know. While we do that we might as well follow Howard and Sean's lead."

Rachael handed Jane her notebook and Jane watched her as she took the seat between her and Bert. She looked across at Lydia.

"Do you really think one of us killed Simon?" Lydia asked. "I mean I know he wasn't an easy man at times, but to kill him..."

"I can't think how else the fatal injury occurred," Jane said. "But let's go through the facts and work out what happened." Jane picked up another piece of chicken and flicked open the notebook. "Let's start with what you found, Lydia."

The woman looked at Jane with empty eyes.

"Janey, why don't you note what Theo and I saw? I don't think Lydia is up to questions right now," Rachael suggested.

"First can I just ask, how many of the people around this table truly liked Simon?" Jane asked.

Nobody caught her eye. "Just as I thought," she said.

"Well, I didn't really know him." Ryan offered. "Although I know him by reputation, and that wasn't great."

Howard laughed. "That's an understatement."

"And I haven't been going to the group long, I didn't know him well either," Theo said.

"You've been going longer than I have," Rachael said.

"Okay, don't argue. It's as I thought," Jane said. "Paula, you saw Simon immediately after Lydia found him. What did you see?"

"I did. I thought she was mistaken about poor Simon's condition. I thought he had, perhaps fallen into a deep sleep after the walk earlier and then I saw the wound. His throat was cut open. It was so awful. And the blood."

"Did you see a knife?" Jane asked.

"No, but the largest knife was missing from the kitchen. That's part of the reason that jointing the chicken was so hard." Theo commented. "Although it was in the sink when I brought the chicken through just now, so maybe I missed it."

"Or maybe the killer put it there."

Lydia gasped. She began crying again.

"Oh Lydia, dear. Would you like to go to you room?" Sylvia asked.

Lydia's sobs became a howl.

"She can't do that," Howard said. "Simon's lying in there dead."

"Oh God!" Lydia whispered. "He's really dead."

"There's a room up on the second floor. Why don't I go upstairs and see if it's been made up. Lydia could use that room while we work things out and when the snow stops we can get help." Rachael suggested.

"Thanks, Rache. Do that please." Jane nodded. "Theo, what did you see when you went into Lydia and Simon's room."

"It was horrible. His throat was cut from ear to ear. Who could possibly have done that? It takes enough strength to joint a chicken."

"I think we're talking about something a bit more serious than jointing a chicken, Theo." Bert whispered.

"Jane, that room is all made up. Shall Paula and I help Lydia up? I think she needs to rest."

"Yes, please could you do that, Rache?"

Rachael and Paula helped Lydia to her feet and guided her to the other bedroom.

"Perhaps I could just go around the table and ask everybody about their relationship with Simon and what they remember about today? Howard let's start with you. I know you and Cynthia are neighbours of Simon and Lydia's, but you and Simon didn't get on," Jane said.

"That's all true, but I didn't kill him."

"Of course you didn't, dear, nobody's saying you did. But since Simon used his council position to decline our planning application for the extension, and everything, you've never really forgiven him, have you?"

"Could you tell me a bit more about that, Cynthia?" Jane asked.

"That's Lydia asleep. I don't know for how long." Paula said. Shall Rachael and I make tea and coffee?"

"Good idea," Sylvia said. "Let's sit in more comfortable chairs."

"I'd rather we sat where we are, while I hear from everyone. I want to look at people directly."

"Cynthia, you were saying."

"We had a daughter, Penelope. She's a lovely girl, but innocent, you could say. She couldn't live on her own. Learning difficulties, they call it now. So we planned to convert the garage and build an extension above it for her."

Howard went on. "But Simon didn't want the extension, said it would invade his privacy. Bloody nonsense! So he spoke to someone in the planning department. Permission was refused. We couldn't afford to appeal the decision, so it never went ahead."

"Penelope got so frustrated. She hated living with us more as she got older. Every month that went passed she would ask when she could move out."

"One day she ran away. She got run over by a car on Morningside Road. Penelope died in hospital. She didn't stand a chance."

"Neither did the driver. She ran out in front of him." Cynthia added. "He was so guilt-ridden he committed suicide."

Howard stared angrily at Jane. "Simon was responsible for both deaths in my eyes. I didn't kill him, but I won't condemn the person who did."

Jane finished taking her notes about all that Howard and Cynthia had to say.

"I'm sorry about your daughter but you certainly had motive."

Rachael and Paula put the tea and coffee on the table and took their seats. Jane watched everyone help themselves to drinks before she poured herself a cup of tea and then recommenced her interviews.

"You're right about that knife Theo, it was in the sink. It's been rinsed, but I've wrapped it in clingfilm, Janey. We may get prints off it. It didn't look like it had been wiped."

"Thanks Rache. And thanks to you and Paula for getting these drinks. I don't think we want to drink too much alcohol with a murderer in our midst," Jane said.

"Theo, you and Ryan both said you didn't know Simon well. How long have you known him?"

"I've been going to the book group for about a year, I suppose," Theo said.

"But you knew him before that," Sean commented. "I saw you refuse to serve him one day in the coffee shop. It was before you joined us, but I remember it, because it was so unusual. I've never seen it happen in any coffee place before or since."

"Theo?" Jane looked at the young man. She saw him blush. "How long have you known Simon and why did you dislike him so much that you wouldn't even serve him coffee?"

"Just tell them, Theo." Ryan said. "It's history now."

"I was working in the council as a young solicitor. I hadn't come out, but somehow Simon found out, or guessed I'm gay."

"Nice," Rachael said. "Did he bully you because of your sexuality? That's illegal!"

"My sexuality, because I'm black, because I'm overweight. Anything that made me different."

"What a bastard!"

"Yeh, Rachael, he was. At first it was just snide comments. But then I was put forward for promotion by my boss."

Jane saw Theo had tears in his eyes.

"Simon had a word with him. Suggested I wouldn't be a suitable candidate. Couldn't have me represent the council at tribunals. You know the sort of thing. You and Rachael must have come across this."

"Not in Police Scotland. We have been blessed with excellent superior officers."

"You're lucky." Ryan rubbed Theo's shoulder. "Simon was a prejudiced bully. That's why Theo had his breakdown. We'll get through this, but it makes it more difficult for us to adopt too, because the breakdown is on Theo's medical record."

"I'm still in therapy. I hate that man so much, but I didn't kill him, however much I applaud the person who did." Theo wiped his eyes and poured himself another coffee.

"So you had motive too."

Rachael turned to Jane. "When we were on our way back from our walk, Sean referred to Simon as evil."

"Evil, Sean? That's a strong word. Why did you use it to describe Simon?"

"Well, I took it back as soon as I said it. Rachael will tell you that."

"Never mind Rachael, what was your experience of Simon that made you refer to him as evil?"

"You said it was something to do with getting money for libraries when he was in the council," Rachael said.

"Rachael, may I hear from Sean?"

Rachael blushed. She looked down and then glowered at Jane before whispering to Howard that she would like another cup of tea. He poured it for her.

Jane ignored all of this and stared at Sean.

"It wasn't just the money. Although he always claimed to be a man of the people."

"Huh! Only if the people were like him," Howard said.

"Exactly," Theo sniffed. He used his paper napkin to wipe his nose.

"Libraries are most important for those less fortunate and more vulnerable in society. You know, poorer families whose kids need the books and computers to do homework, older folk who stop in to be with other people and read the papers or the unemployed who want to borrow books or use the computers to look for jobs."

"Yes, yes, Sean." Jane sounded dismissive. "We get the point, so what made you refer to Simon as evil. It wasn't poor library funding, was it?"

"Not just that, no."

"So, what was it?"

"Oh for God's sake, just tell them, Sean." Sylvia said.

"Simon is my stepbrother. His mother married my father when I and my twin sister were seven and Simon was thirteen. He had been the centre of his mother's world since his parent's divorced when he was a baby and didn't take to sharing her too well."

"What happened to your mother?" Jane asked.

"She died giving birth to us. It was hard on Dad."

"It would be, but none of that makes Simon evil."

"No. It was raping my sister week in and week out and making me watch that made him evil."

Jane was silent. She didn't know what to say. Sean certainly had a reason to have killed Simon. She glanced at Rachael. Her wife had tears rolling down her cheeks, but she knew they weren't just for Sean, but also in acknowledgement of Jane's own difficult early life in care. She frowned at Rachael. Jane didn't want to go there right now.

Rachael stood up. "Can I make more tea and coffee and bring through the cheese. We must all be hungry by now."

"I'll help you," Paula said.

Jane nodded at Rachael and then shifted her gaze to Sylvia and Bert. "Last but not least. How did you feel about Simon."

Sylvia smiled, "You haven't guessed?"

"Guessed what?" Jane asked.

"My memory isn't what it used to be, but I'll never forget Simon and what he did. I'm Sean's twin sister."

"Oh God! You have the best reason of all," Jane said. "Rachael didn't tell me that."

"Why should she? I doubt she knows. Simon knew, and Lydia of course, Sean and Paula, naturally but did anybody else know?"

"Not at all," Cynthia said. "Of course it was Paula who suggested you might join, but she never said you're related. Why did you never tell us?"

Paula walked into the room. "It wasn't my story to tell, nor would I. Anyway, it was never relevant, I wanted you to get to know Sylvia and Bert on their own merit." She smiled at Sylvia. "Here's the cheese and crackers, I'll get the fresh pot of coffee now."

"Rache, did you know Sylvia and Sean were twins?"

"No, I didn't know, Janey. Don't sound so accusing. Oh God, it was you!"

"Yes, it was me." Sylvia nodded. "Life was difficult for a long time, until I met Bert. He saved my life, literally."

"Oh, I wouldn't say that, but we're happy to be together." Bert took Sylvia's hand and kissed it. "I'm a lucky man to have met you."

"We met when I was nursing in Uganda."

"You had a wee bit of trouble and ended up in hospital, didn't you?"

"What Bert means is that I made a suicide attempt, and he was the hospital chaplain. He spent hours talking to me until I could start to put my past behind me."

"It was love at first sight, I couldn't let you go, darling." Bert smiled adoringly at his wife. "And I never will."

"I know, dear, I know. I also know neither of us killed that wicked man, no matter the provocation. You don't have the will and I don't have the strength."

Jane cut a chunk of brie off the large slice she and Rachael brought and picked up a couple of crackers from the plate. She shook her head and gazed around the room. Every couple around the table had an extremely good reason for wanting Simon dead, but which of them could inflict such a deadly wound? It would take strength to cut through Simon's neck like that and he would have to be out for the count for the wound to be inflicted.

She suddenly noticed that there was silence around the table as the group tucked into the cheese. She decided not to break the quiet but took more cheese to chew on while she thought.

So if everyone had a motive, who had opportunity? That was the next issue. She reached for the pot of tea and poured herself another cup. Lydia and Simon had arrived first, so nobody else could have set any kind of trap or laid a plan to murder Simon.

She frowned and glanced at Rachael.

"What are you thinking Janey?"

"I'm thinking that if everyone except us knew Simon and had a reason to want to get back at him, who had the opportunity?"

"Okay, let's talk that through."

"Simon must have been sedated because nobody could have inflicted that wound unless he was out cold."

"So who had time with Simon, before he went for his lie down?" Rachael asked as she looked around the group.

"You did," Theo said.

"Did I? Oh yes, we walked together on the way out. But all I did was walk and listen."

"Maybe, but the question was, who had time with him," Cynthia said.

"Who did he walk back with?" Rachael asked.

"He walked at the front with me and Theo," Bert said. "But like you, we walked and listened." He looked at Rachael.

"What happened when we all got back? We had drinks and biscuits, didn't we?" Jane asked.

"Yes. I put the biscuits on the plate and put out the milk and sugar and almost everyone used the milk and sugar," Howard said

"I made the tea," Cynthia said. "But I couldn't have put anything in the tea, or you would all be doped."

"I wouldn't, I had Lydia's lemonade," Ryan said.

"Who had tea and who had lemonade?" Jane asked.

"Lydia, Ryan, Bert, and I had lemonade," Rachael said.

"Simon did too. Lydia lent over me to hand him his glass first, I thought it was a bit rude," Bert said.

"Hmm. Did everyone else have tea?"

"Yes. And the biscuits were wrapped, so they were safe," Howard said.

"Did Simon have anything else to eat or drink?" Jane asked.

"Not that I remember," Paula said.

"No, I don't think any of us did until drinks before dinner, but he wasn't with us for that."

"He was probably dead by then." Jane said. "Did he take any tablets?"

"I remember Lydia saying he took a sleeping tablet at night, otherwise he didn't sleep."

"*He* didn't sleep! That's rich." Theo said.

"So either there were sleeping tablets in his lemonade, or he took them himself or someone hit him on the head to knock him out." Jane breathed out deeply. "I didn't notice him bleeding from anywhere except his neck, did anybody else?"

Rachael, Paula, and Theo all shook their heads.

"Theo, would you please come through with me and check if there is any evidence of Simon having been hit on the head before he was murdered?"

"Why not me?" Rachael asked.

"I want a witness, but I want you here to make sure nobody else leaves."

"Well, I'm going to need to go to the bathroom sooner rather than later," Howard said.

"Of course." Jane smiled.

"Please let everybody use your bathroom and go through one at a time. You can be gatekeeper, Rache."

"I get all the good jobs." Rachael grimaced.

"Come on, you're with me, Theo. Everyone else, bathroom break."

"Is she always this bossy?" Cynthia asked Rachael.

"This is her being polite."

When the meeting at the table resumed, Jane and Theo confirmed that neither of them could see or feel any evidence of Simon having a bump on the head or a head wound.

"So from that, I deduce Simon was sleeping so deeply either because he took or was given his sleeping tablets."

There was a creak on the stairs. Everybody turned round and Lydia was stood on the stairs.

"Lydia, dear. How long have you been there?" Paula asked. "How are you? Did you get some sleep? It's all too terrible, isn't it? Jane is trying to help by working out how Simon died."

"He didn't die. He was killed." Lydia turned to Jane. "Do you know who did it yet?"

"Not yet, Lydia, but it does seem that your husband was rather unpopular within the group. Did you know that everyone in the book group had a reason to loathe Simon?"

"Oh yes, he would boast about how he couldn't go because everyone had an axe to grind."

"That's rich," Bert said. "The man was a monster!"

"He'd always tell me that you all bore grudges and he couldn't change the past."

"No he can't, but he could have worked on being a kinder person going forward," Theo said.

"My husband can't work on anything, he's dead. So which of you lot killed him?"

"Come on Lydia! Do you really think any of us is capable of murder?" Howard asked.

"Don't answer that, Lydia," Jane said. "Are you hungry or do you need anything to eat?"

Lydia shook her head. "I'm not hungry, but maybe I'll take a coffee. I feel so woolly headed. I just can't believe Simon's dead. It feels unreal."

Paula handed her the coffee. Lydia added milk.

"Was Simon a good husband?" Jane asked. "Did you have a happy marriage?"

"Gosh, you don't beat around the bush, do you? What is a good husband? Is any marriage happy?" She sipped her coffee and stared at the table.

"Let me make it simpler," Jane said. "How did Simon behave around you?"

"Lydia just tell her," Sean shouted. "Simon was a bully, and it didn't matter whether it was Theo, Sylvia, me, or you, he was nasty. Tell her what he did to you."

"You tell her, or I will," Cynthia said.

"It's not your place, to say anything, any of you."

"But you complained to us every month when we met. You said we were your safety net."

"Going to the book group was the only thing he allowed you to do on your own, and that was next door to where you live." Theo said. "It must have been so claustrophobic."

"It was hell." Lydia agreed. She looked at Jane. "At first, when we got together, we were young. I thought it was lovely that Simon was protective of me. We did everything together, and that's the way I wanted it. I wanted to be with him all the time, every moment."

"Did that change?" Jane asked.

"Well, yes. In the beginning, I had a job at the council, I was a secretary and Simon was a young councillor. So glamorous and exciting, and we both had our own wages. I was head over heels in love, although the girls in the office did warn me he had a bad temper, I never saw it."

"We got married and quickly had our first, Simone. She was a lovely little girl, but she had a genetic disease and died when she was only two. It broke my heart. We had a son, Simon junior the year after Simone's death. But he had the same thing. He died at only one year old. I was inconsolable. I was seriously ill with depression."

"I'm not surprised," Rachael whispered.

"Simon changed towards me after that. He kept saying it was my fault because it was mitochondrial disease. It's only passed by the mother, you see." Lydia started to cry. "I couldn't work. I had no money, and he controlled all our cash coming in. I had to ask for things like tights and personal items to be added to the shopping list. It was demeaning." She sobbed. "My self-esteem went through the floor. He told me people didn't like me, I couldn't conduct a conversation, we only got invited places because of him."

"But you knew that wasn't true. The book group included you but didn't want him there." Rachael looked amazed.

"That's logical, when you're depressed you don't think logically," Theo said.

"That's true." Jane frowned. "Lydia, do you take any tablets?"

Lydia laughed. "I take daytime anti-depressants, night-time anti-depressants, sleeping tablets, you name it, I take it. The pills don't help."

"Simon took sleeping tablets too, you said. Please could I see the tablets both of you take?"

"They're in that room." She nodded towards the room where Simon's body lay.

"Okay, are they tablets or capsules?"

"We both take capsules."

"So you can open them and empty out the contents?"

"Yes, but it tastes terrible. I'd never want to do that."

"You've tasted the medication then? Strongly flavoured home-made lemonade would disguise the taste, I'd guess."

"Janey, what are you suggesting?"

"I'm suggesting that the person with the strongest reason to murder Simon was his own wife. She also had the opportunity to take the knife when she made the lemonade and return it when she got Simon's whisky. Didn't you, Lydia?" Jane turned to the woman.

"You endured years of abuse. You took your chance when Rachael suggested a walk and made up the lemonade with the fruit brought for our drinks. Added lots of sugar and put enough sleeping medication into Simon's glass. You were careful to serve him first, so he got the glass you wanted him to have. You were onto a fairly safe bet that he'd feel tired, go to lie down and you must have given him enough medication that he would sleep through almost anything.

"Did you get blood on your jumper? Is that why you changed? Even though it was bright red, blood is quite a different colour, especially as it dries. Lydia, did you kill Simon?"

"Bastard got what he deserved. I only wish I'd done it years ago." Lydia spat out the words and everybody around the table knew what she said was true.

. . .

I had never been here before. I have never had to be here before. But I was laid off and it smells. Being laid off doesn't smell, that stinks. Last in first out. Who cares if I was good at my job and old Bob they kept on is an alcoholic kleptomaniac who makes unwanted passes at the girls. He has been there twenty years, so he stays, and I go.

No, it's the jobcentre that smells even as I approach it, walking anxiously from the bus stop. The stench of the cruel and unusual punishment that is claiming benefits wafts its way towards me. The smell is of dirt and dust and despair.

The doors open automatically as I approach. They close behind me swallowing me whole. I stop and look around. This causes the two guys behind me to trip over me and a third one with endless tattoos to use a word I had never heard before, but I guess what it means and move a little further into the abyss.

Everybody knows where they are going except me.

A chubby man with grey hair, glasses and a badge around his neck tutted at me and signalled me to come over to him.

"You can't stand there," he said. "Where you going?"

"I don't know. I have an appointment at 11."

"Which section?"

"I don't know."

He sighs dramatically and waves towards the sweaty papers scrunched up in my hands. I relinquish them to his fat fist and he glances at them and looks at his watch.

"You're early. They're running late. Section B."

"They're always running fucking late. Arrive 10 minutes early is a fucking one-way street." Growled the man with the vocabulary and the tattoos.

"Where did you find section B?" I whispered to the chubby one.

He pulled a face that indicated the level of idiot he was used to dealing with was not quite as dim as me. He pointed to a microscopic 'B' in the bottom right-hand corner of the page.

I admitted to having missed that and he grunted, acknowledging my stupidity as he returned the squashed papers. He waved me away towards the melee of hopelessness that surrounded him, and now me.

I sat beside the man with tattoos. He smiled at me, and I couldn't help wondering what I'd have to give him to dispense with Bob so I could get my job back.

IN PLAIN SIGHT

SATURDAY 18TH JUNE 1988

MICK LOOKED AT HIS DAUGHTER AND SMILED. WHERE HAD THE years gone? She stood on the stairs, grinning from ear to ear, so grown up in the pink dress and high heeled shoes that she and her mother had chosen. Martha walked over to her husband and followed the direction of his gaze to admire their first born, their girl.

Mick could hear their twin sons, Leroy and Jethro giggling from the living room. Not all the children had grown up yet.

"Will I do?" Babs asked.

"You look stunning, honey," Her Mom said.

"Beautiful," Mick agreed. "When is this Jerome calling for you?"

"He should be here any minute now. Oh, gosh, I forgot my lipstick, I'll just be a minute. If he comes when I'm upstairs, Dad, be nice."

"I'm always nice."

"Well, don't tell any of your jokes."

"I can't promise *that* baby girl."

"And don't call me that! I'm eighteen now."

"Eighteen today." Martha smiled at Mick. "How did we get from diapers to lipstick so quick?"

"Damned if I know."

The doorbell rang and Mick raced to get to the door first.

"Good evening, Mr Potter, I'm Jerome Sheriff. I'm here to take Barbara to the prom if it's all right with you."

"And if it's not?"

His sons laughed at their dad's question.

"That's enough, boys. Go and play in the yard. Take no notice, Jerome," Martha said. We're so pleased to meet you. You look very handsome, dear. Is that a new tux?"

"No, I hired it for the weekend, ma'am. It has to go back on Monday."

"Well, it's a good fit and you look very smart. And what a nice car."

"I bought a fixer upper and got it running myself. I like mending cars."

"So does Mick, so much so, he made a career out of it." She smiled and then called up to her daughter, "Babs, Jerome is here."

Babs appeared at the top of the stairs and rushed down to greet her date, carrying her shoes in her left hand. Only then did Mick notice her painted toenails. Nail polish and lipstick, good lord, his baby girl really had grown up.

"Good evening, Babs," Jerome said. "You look lovely. I bought you this pink corsage, I hope you like it."

"It's perfect. Thank you, Jerome. Isn't it beautiful, Dad?"

"Indeed. Well, you both have a good time and be home by midnight."

"Aw, Dad, maybe just a little later?"

"Ask again and your curfew will be eleven."

"It's no problem, Mr Potter. The prom finishes at eleven, I'll have Babs safely home by midnight, don't you worry."

"But I will worry until she's home."

"Yes, sir. I'll take care of her."

. . .

Jerome drove through the streets of Charlottesville until they got to Renaissance High School. As captain of the football team, Jerome made a short speech before he and Babs danced every dance together. They chatted with friends, enjoyed the food, and learned that their friends Andy Wright and his girlfriend, Lilian would be joining them at the University of Virginia.

"What's your major?" Lilian asked Babs.

"Landscape Architecture, but Jerome is going to major in accountancy. What about you?"

Lilian squealed, "Andy is doing accountancy too. That's epic. I'm enrolling in design. We can hang out together at college. That's neat."

15th May 1992

"Mom, will you please tell my father that I am going to the party Andy's dad is throwing for graduation and I'm going with Jerome. He can like it or lump it."

"No, dear. I suggest that if you have something to say to your father, you tell him yourself."

"Martha, will you tell your daughter that I don't like that boy, I have never liked that Andy Wright, I don't trust his father and I don't want Babs anywhere near their home."

"It's a bit late now, Dad. We've been hanging out at university for four years."

"Yes, in daylight, with other people around. I don't like it, Babs, I don't like it one bit."

The doorbell interrupted them. Martha opened the door to Jerome.

"I waited for a pause before I rang the bell," he told her. "I didn't think you'd hear me otherwise."

"You were probably right," Martha said.

"I'll take good care of her, Mr. Potter, I always have, and I always will, as far as I'm able."

"I know, son. You're a good man."

"Which brings me to another thing I'd been going to ask you, sir."

Mick looked at Jerome quizzically.

"I'd like your permission for Barbara's hand in marriage."

"You don't need his permission, Jerome," Babs said. "What about mine?"

"But it's mighty fine that he's asked, and I think you'd be damn lucky to have a young man like that by your side. If Babs won't have you, I'll marry you myself!" Mick joked and shook Jerome by the hand. "Welcome to the family, son."

Jerome smiled and got down on one knee, "Barbara Potter, will you make me the happiest man alive and do me the honour of agreeing to become my wife." He took a small box out of his pocket and opened it to reveal a diamond solitaire ring. He slipped the ring on her finger. "I've been saving up for this since our high school prom," he said.

Babs and Jerome were dazzled by the undisguised wealth on show at the party. Grapefruit negroni was served in hollowed out blush grapefruits, daiquiris in coconut shells and mai tais were drunk from pineapple skins. The guests danced around the pool to the music provided by Mariah Carey and Prince while canapes and champagne were offered by waiters in black outfits until the buffet was served. Babs pointed to the card which showed that the celebrity chef, Wolfgang Puck supplied the catering.

"This must have cost a fortune," Babs said.

"I know. Mr Wright is the senior partner in his accountancy firm, but I'm amazed that it's quite so grand."

"Perhaps you should have accepted his offer to join the firm."

"Perhaps, but I think I'll get a good grounding in all aspects of accounting and forensic accounting at the bank."

"Forensic accounting sounds very dull," Babs smiled.

"Maybe it does, but it's what I need to know to catch the fraudsters and embezzlers."

Babs smiled at Jerome. "I'm going to show Andy and Lilian my ring. Will you get us some more drinks?"

He kissed her gently on the lips and wandered to the bar.

"Having a good time?" Andy slapped Jerome on the shoulder and draped his arm around him and they walked towards the bar.

"Indeed I am. This was a fine party."

"Saw you got a bit of glitter for your lady. Congratulations. I would like to have a ride on her before you tie the knot, if you don't mind," Andy said.

Jerome shook his arm from his shoulder. "You what? I just hope you are too drunk to know what you're saying. That's disgusting."

"Oh, go on, I wouldn't really damage the goods, just a little brown sugar for a pal. I've never tried it and I need to taste."

Jerome stood with his fists clenched and his mouth set into a hard line.

"Go on, hit me, pal. Do it and my dad will see that you never work within five hundred miles of here, boy." Andy's smile didn't meet his eyes.

Jerome checked his temper and walked away to find Babs. She and Lilian were still admiring her engagement ring and were discussing venues.

"We have to leave."

"Why, I'd like to stay and dance a while," Babs said. She snuggled up to Jerome and looked so hurt when he shrugged off her grasp.

"We're leaving, Babs. Enjoy the rest of your evening, Lilian. Please thank Mr Wright for inviting us."

Their wedding day was perfect. Babs looked beautiful, her young brothers were honoured to be Jerome's groomsmen, and her cousin Hattie was a lovely bridesmaid. Jerome's mother sat with Babs's mum and both shed happy tears as she walked down the aisle on her dad's arm. The church choir sang. Nobody could remember a happier occasion.

When Babs and Jerome left the reception, there was great speculation as to where they were going for their honeymoon. They had told nobody, but that didn't stop some of the guests believing they would go to Acapulco in Mexico, while others thought they had gone hiking in Canada and yet more thought the couple had flown to Las Vegas and one of the luxury hotels.

Not one person mentioned New Orleans, but Jerome and Babs had carefully planned their wedding date so that they could be in the Big Easy for Mardi Gras. They particularly wanted to see the Zulu parade and had managed to book a room in the Bourbon Orleans Hotel near Jackson Square. Jerome bought Babs a single red rose from the tiny flower shop on the corner of the square. They saw the parade from the very beginning and followed it around the city, enjoying the camaraderie, costumes, and music.

"What a wonderful day," Babs said. She held Jerome's hand. "I'm so pleased we came here."

"I agree, there may be many parades during Mardi Gras, but this is the one I most wanted to see." He kissed her gently and then said, "I would be happy having dinner in the hotel, what do you think?"

"I'm so glad you said that. I'm goosed. Shall we try the creole restaurant?"

"Great idea. Let's get back to the hotel and we'll shower and change before we eat."

August 1997

The next five years passed quickly. Jerome's reputation and numerical skill allowed him to rise steadily through the ranks of the accountancy department at the bank. Babs loved her work at Making Landscapes Matter. She had two spells of maternity leave. During those times she and Jerome welcomed Michael, who was named after her dad and Rosie-Lee the most good-natured child ever. Her joy was tempered by the sudden death of her father, but the children remained the focus of the family and her mother and Jerome's mom shared childcare duties to allow Babs to return to work.

She never took the grandmas for granted but was glad she had not had to give up her career. She was always happiest meeting with clients and carrying out the initial survey before putting together a plan that she thought would meet their requirements. This afternoon was no different.

There are many fabulous homes in Charlottesville and today Babs was travelling up the long drive to the new clients' elegant mansion in Rugby Road. She knew, however hard she and Jerome worked, they could never afford to buy a home like this. Designing the garden was as close as she could hope to get. Babs stepped out of her car and noticed the infinity pool down the side of the house. Neat. The clients wanted a four seasons garden around their home in the middle of the twelve acres of ground. This would be a lovely job.

She rang the doorbell and was not surprised that it had an inbuilt security device that photographed her.

"I'll be right there," a voice said.

Babs saw a woman coming towards her in tennis gear. When she was close enough to recognise her, she threw down her racket and ran towards her.

"Babs!" she shouted. "Is it really you?"

"Lilian?"

"Yes, after all these years. We never heard from you after Jerome left Andy's party so suddenly. He was very odd that night. We didn't even get an invite to your wedding, so of course, I couldn't invite you to ours. But it's so good to see you. Wait till I tell Andy that you're our landscaper. He'll be thrilled. We were all so close at college, I'm glad we've caught up with you again." Lilian threw her arms around Babs. "Now let's go inside and get a drink, I'm gasping.

Water, iced tea or freshly squeezed lemonade? It's much too hot for coffee, isn't it?"

Babs smiled. "Iced tea would be lovely, thank you."

She allowed Lilian to take her arm and lead her into the house. The kitchen was huge. It was bigger than the living room and kitchen combined in Babs's house. The white units and tiled floor gleamed. The sun streamed through the glass doors that looked out onto the tennis court. A fit young man sat in the corner of the court fiddling with his tennis racket and a yellow Lamborghini sat outside the triple garage.

"Now you must tell me all about what you've been up to," Lilian said. She passed Babs a glass of iced tea and poured one for herself before returning the pitcher to the fridge. "Andy was made partner at his dad's firm last year. His gramps died. So sad."

"It must have been, He wasn't really an old man, was he?"

"Seventy-two. So of course, the firm needed a new partner, but they have so much work, I hardly ever see Andy. Lucky, I have somewhere decent to live."

"It seems more than decent to me; you have a beautiful home."

"Well, it will be a lot better when we get the garden area looking good. Let's go and take a walk around the grounds and you can tell me your ideas."

Babs picked up her notebook and followed Lilian into the area they wanted to turn into a kitchen garden. She began suggesting raised beds for herbs and spices when Lilian spoke again.

"Yes, that sounds good. I want mostly vegetables and soft fruits. Do you think we need a greenhouse? I thought it might be a good idea for the plants when they were young or seedlings or whatever you call them, the head gardener did tell me. Anyway, let's go further. Four seasons, I thought."

"Do you want this bit to be child friendly?"

"Oh, God no!" Lilian laughed. "I won't keep this figure by having kids, will I?"

Babs looked at Lilian's tiny waist and athletic legs and replied, "I guess not."

"How many you got? Two? Let me guess a boy and a girl."

Babs nodded.

"It'll cost you a fortune to get them through college now. We don't plan any kids." She walked on. "In this part I'd like a pergola and a nice Japanesey feel. We went to Japan on our honeymoon."

"We went to New Orleans for Mardi Gras."

"In Spring, Japan is beautiful. All the cherry blossoms. Have you been? The food is marvellous too. When we're entertaining, I usually get the chef from *Now and Zen* to cater. Have you been? The food is excellent, and the service is discrete."

Babs continued making notes in her book and followed Lilian, jotting down her client's requirements as they made their way to the lake at the far end of the grounds.

"I thought a couple of rowing boats would be nice, but the lake will need to be dredged. Now is there anything else you need to know?" Lilian paused for breath.

"If you need any extra information, you can call me, dear, or speak to Isaac."

"Isaac?"

"The head gardener. It's been lovely to catch up and learn all about what you and Jerome have been doing. You must come over for dinner. Saturday, come on Saturday. Do say you'll come, and we'll have Japanese. You said how much you like it." Lilian smiled at Babs. "Well, here we are back at your car. Gosh a Chevvy Spark. I've not seen one of those for a while."

"Jerome bought it at an auction and fixed it up. That's his hobby."

"Very nice, Babs. Well, I'm glad it's you doing the grounds. See you Saturday. Shall we say seven for seven thirty? Looking forward to it already. Bye, dear."

With that, Lilian turned her back and jogged back towards the tennis court. "Bobby, I'm going to thrash you this time."

. . .

"No, please no. Don't say you accepted. We've managed to avoid Andy for all these years, and you end up working on his grounds and get us invited to dinner. I really, really don't want to go."

"I didn't accept. I hardly got to say anything. She just talked non-stop and then said how lovely it was to catch up, but it would be worth accepting the invitation just for you to see their home."

"I could go visit a show home and not have to spend time with Andy."

"Look, that was years ago, and he was drunk, we were all friends for such a long time. Maybe it would be nice to catch up."

"I bet it's not."

"Look, love, how many annual bank dances have I suffered for you? Dinners with managers and directors to help your career. Please would you do this for me and come to Andy and Lilian's for dinner and be nice?"

"When you put it like that, how can I not?" He drew her into his arms and kissed her deeply.

"Oh no, Mum and Dad are kissing again. Don't look, Michael, it's the kissing bit." Rosie-Lee covered her eyes and ran away giggling.

"You have crazy kids, but they are very cute," Jerome said.

"Funnily enough, so are yours. So, dinner on Saturday?"

"It's a date. I'll get my mom to babysit."

"Thank you darling. Now, where are those kids? I'm going to find them and kiss them." Babs ran out of the back door, into the yard and chased the giggling Rosie-Lee until she caught and kissed her."

"You won't catch me, Mum," Michael called.

"Don't bet on it, big boy!"

The kids squealed and Babs laughed. Jerome stood in the doorway. Who needed twelve acres of land when you had a loving family?

. . .

After dinner, Lilian and Babs moved into the living room while Andy poured Jerome another large brandy.

"You know, I really respected you that night at the graduation party. What an ass I was back then."

"That was a long time ago, forget it, Andy."

"No, I was drunk and trying it on, but you wouldn't have it. You didn't hit me either. Respect."

Jerome smiled. "I came close. But it's all water under the bridge."

"I'm glad you say that. I hear you're the best forensic accountant at the bank. That's quite an accolade."

"I do my best."

"What I'm getting at is my firm needs your skills. Since my gramps died, we've not had a forensic specialist, and we want the best."

"That's flattering, Andy, but I'm happy at the bank and I'm in line for promotion next year."

"Please don't say no. You'll come in as an associate, partner in five years, named partner in ten."

"Really, Andy, it's kind, but no. I like where I am. I start at eight in the morning, finish at six in the evening and go home to my family. I'm happy."

"Whatever they're paying you, we'll multiply it by ten, but we might multiply your hours by ten too."

Jerome laughed. "That's not possible and it's silly money."

"And you'll have thirty days paid vacation every year."

"You've got to be kidding. Those terms are incredible."

"Tell me you'll think about it?"

"I'd be crazy not to. When do you need to know?"

"Eight on Monday morning, otherwise the offer will go to the next best candidate, but I don't want them. I want you."

. . .

"He offered you how much? And you had to think about it? Jerome. You should have bitten his hand off."

"I like to think things through."

"What's to think? We could pay off the mortgage and put so much away for the kids that they can go to any college they want."

"So why do they want me. I'm good, but I'm only a bank accountant."

"A forensic accountant, the best the bank's ever had. The directors told you that. You can retire early, we can travel. Please Jerome. Take the job. I'll never forgive you if you don't."

"I'd have much longer hours, travel to meet with important clients. You get nothing for nothing, pet. I'll sleep on it."

"Jerome, good to see you. Let me show you around. Have you got a drink? I'll take you to the coffee spot first."

"Starbucks. Impressive, Andy. I do like my coffee. I think I'll be happy here."

"I'll make sure of it, and if you ever leave, I'll make sure you're miserable anywhere else. Believe it. Dad's firm is like Hotel California, no one ever leaves, except in a wooden box. Now let me introduce you to some people."

Jerome was introduced to more people than he had met in a long time. "Couldn't they all wear name tags? It would make my life a lot easier."

"You're not here for an easy life, boy. Now, let's grab my dad and get a bite of lunch with him."

Jerome sat in the country club feeling hugely uncomfortable. There were no prices on his menu because his was a guest menu. He chose the sea bass and water to drink.

"Have a glass of wine, my boy, this is a celebration," Mr Wright said.

"No thanks, I need a clear head for going back to the office."

Jerome listened as his hosts ordered the surf and turf and a bottle of Chateau Neuf du Pape before returning their menus to the waiter. It was only then that he caught the expression on the man's face. He noticed that, apart from the staff, his was the only black face in the room. This issue never arose in the bank, his colleagues represented all colours, creeds, and orientations. Jerome had liked it that way. He knew that life at Mr Wright's firm would be different, but he hadn't thought of this.

"Now, before our meals arrive, let's get down to business," Mr Wright said. "You know we were keen to secure your services, Jerome. I hope you have been made to feel welcome."

"Yes, Mr Wright, thank you."

The drinks arrived and the waiter served the wine, but just placed the water jug in front of Jerome on the table.

Mr Wright cleared his throat. "A little more service is required here, Anton," he said loudly to the head waiter.

"Of course, Mr Wright. I can't think what Peter was thinking." He poured the water himself. "Let me know if I may be of further assistance. He stormed off towards the kitchen carrying the jug. Raised voices, followed by a loud screech were heard before Peter emerged from the kitchen, dripping wet and carrying his coat.

The man glared at Jerome and as he walked by said one word, "Coconut."

"I think the club will be a better place without that young man," Mr Wright said. "Now, back to business. Andy will have told you that your days of conventional office hours are over, hasn't he?"

"He indicated that, yes sir."

"Good, because tomorrow you'll come up to New York with me to meet one of our wealthiest clients. He's a musician, a rapper, Angry Poppa he calls himself, his real name is Junior Smith, but apparently that's not sufficiently rock and roll."

"Rap isn't much rock and roll either, Dad," Andy said. He grinned at Jerome, making sure he had appreciated the joke.

"You be at the Delta desk at the airport at six tomorrow morning, and we'll be on the seven o'clock flight to La Guardia. I've got a limo picking us up to take us into the city."

"I'll be there, Mr Wright. Is there anything you need me to bring?"

"A time sheet a notebook and a thick red pen. Junior is thick and likes the colour red."

Andy and his dad laughed heartily.

"Speaking of which, how long has this meeting lasted?" Andy asked.

"About three hours including travel here and back. Call it three twenty, it's less suspicious than a round number," Mr Wright said. "Soon I must introduce you to one of our celebrity chef clients, George Ramsbottom, he's opening more restaurants, and we'll need to sort his books, or he'll be crippled with tax. Anton, I'll need two receipts for the clients' files." Then he winked at Jerome and rose from the table. "Another excellent meal, Anton, same table on Friday." The man marched from the dining room and towards his car.

Jerome arrived at the airport in good time. He waited patiently until Mr Wright appeared, strolling towards him.

"Good morning, Jerome. Now this meeting with Junior today is to accomplish two things, first to introduce you and second, to set up a company network to minimise his taxes." He looked at his watch, then at Jerome. "Our meeting started at six twenty, note that down will you Jerome?" He took the tickets out of his pocket and led the way to the first-class check-in.

"Any luggage, gentlemen?"

"No, we're coming back tonight."

"That's fine. You're in first class and the flight will leave from gate 10."

"I've never flown first class before," Jerome said.

"Better get used to it, boy."

"But it's such a short flight, why do we bother?"

"The client is paying, so why not?"

Jerome walked silently alongside his boss and couldn't help thinking they'd save the client more money if they flew economy and started the meeting when they arrived.

Jerome recognised Angry Poppa as soon as they walked into his suite. He was staying in the Penthouse Suite of the Hilton Towers and there was plenty of space for him to meet with his attorneys and accountants.

"I have a concert tonight, so I'm leaving for the sound-check at three. You boys be all wrapped up by then. What you need from me?"

The retainers demanded of him were more than Jerome would earn in six months, even on his new inflated salary, but the star never blinked, just transferred the cash. Then Jerome sat down beside Mr Wright and opposite the attorneys while shell companies in the Virgin Islands and Bahamas were discussed. The red flags the bank had taught him to be wary of, he was now being encouraged to wave.

It was after nine before he got home. The kids were in bed, but Babs warmed his meal in the microwave, got them each a beer and listened as he recounted the story of his day and his misgivings.

"But these companies aren't anything to do with you, are they?"

"I'm a director along with one of the junior attorneys, April, and she's the secretary too."

"Well, I suppose it'll be okay, after all, Andy's dad is in charge."

"Your dad never liked him, though, did he?"

"No, I miss Dad."

The following week, Jerome accompanied Mr Wright to Los Angeles. They met a British film star, Johnny Darrow, who had recently landed himself the title role in a new detective series and needed accountancy and legal advice "to avoid paying shed loads of tax here and at home," he said as he shook Jerome warmly by the hand.

The meeting took place in a conference room at his hotel. Jerome was surprised to see the same attorneys sitting opposite them at the table.

"We always try to work together," Mr Wright said. "Good to know who's on your side."

Similar companies were set up for Johnny as had been established for Junior, but the retainers demanded were considerably smaller.

On the flight back to Charlottesville, Jerome queried the retainer.

"Oh, that's simple, Jerome, Johnny is only starting out. We've seen his contract and that's as much as he can afford right now. You watch how it will rise next year." The man ordered a large Scotch on the flight and asked for a receipt. Jerome had a water. No receipt required. Old habits die hard.

Jerome was getting used to flying first class, but the early starts and late finishes meant he was seeing less and less of the kids. He found that hard.

Babs had finished the work at Lilian and Andy's house. She was thrilled by how much they complimented her designs and recommended her to their friends. She also went to play tennis with Lilian every Tuesday morning after dropping the kids at school. Her employers agreed Lilian was a good contact to cultivate. All in all, she was beginning to feel part of a new, wealthier group. She got rid of her old Chevvy and replaced it with a brand-new Lincoln.

"I think we should take a vacation," Jerome said. "When the kids' school term finishes, why don't we take a few days and go down to Florida? We can go to Disney World. They'll love it."

"It's all right for you, but I only get ten days off, and that's including public holidays," Babs said.

"Then take the days unpaid. For goodness' sake, pet. Ditch the job if you like. I earn more than enough for both of us now."

"Don't you belittle my job, Jerome Sheriff. I may not earn as much money as you, but I love my job and I can look myself in the mirror. I'm not facilitating the rich beating the system."

"That's not how it is at all, Babs. I play a straight bat, I always have. Look, honey, I must go, but why don't you book us a villa near Disney. It'll be great. But today, I have a flight to catch."

"Of course, you do. Where are you going today?"

"Las Vegas. Mr Wright wants to introduce me to one of our clients who owns a casino. I'll be back tomorrow." He kissed her on the head because she didn't move to return the affection. "See you tomorrow, Babs." He lifted his overnight bag and walked out of the house and towards the cab. "Airport please. And I'll need a receipt to include the tip."

"This a first visit to Sin City for you, boy?" Mr Wright asked as they took their seats.

"Yes, first visit."

"You should come with me to the casino tonight. Classy girls and chance to win a ton of money."

"I have my own classy girl at home, Mr Wight. I'd also guess that far more people lose a ton of money than win it. Thank you but I'll pass. Maybe I can get a ticket to see Penn and Teller. They're funny. Will we see your other chef client, George Ramsbottom while we're in Las Vegas?"

"And waste getting a full fee for another visit? Not likely, Jerome. Now, let's get this deal done."

There was a full day's work on the status of the casino ownership and the myriad of companies and overseas shell companies that would divert profits from the IRS. Jerome was now familiar with the attorneys across the table. When he mentioned that he planned to go and see Penn and Teller that evening the young female attorney mentioned that she would like to go too. They agreed to meet for a bite to eat and shared a cab to the show.

Over dinner, Jerome discovered that April's birthday fell on the same day as his, April first. She used to work in a bank too and as they chatted Jerome became aware that April was concerned about being named as company director and secretary set up for the rich and famous clients of her firm.

"Doesn't it worry you, Jerome?"

"I got uneasy about it when I first started, but I figure if Mr Wright thinks it's okay then it must be."

"But he doesn't take the risks, does he? He's never a director and neither is my boss. You and I are the patsies. If any of our clients were investigated, it would be our necks on the line."

They went on to the Penn and Teller show, but Jerome barely smiled, let alone laughed. He couldn't get April's words out of his head. He didn't sleep that night.

The usual companies and foreign shell companies were set up for the casino owner on the second day of business and when Jerome flew back to Charlottesville, he joined Mr Wright for a Scotch. He remembered to ask for a receipt.

Jerome was exhausted but he didn't sleep that night either. His tossing and turning woke Babs.

"What's wrong pet? You're unusually restless. Is there anything I can help with? Do you want to talk about it?"

Jerome turned to her and repeated what April had said.

"The solution is easy; you have to get in first."

"What on earth do you mean?"

"Gather the information on two or three of the clients to back up your assertions and take it to the IRS. Then leave it to them."

"But I'll lose my job, I'll be struck off, I'll never have enough to send the kids to private college. I'll go to jail. Babs, that way lies madness."

"Yes, you'll lose your job, you'll probably be struck off, but you can do something else. Be a mechanic. Let's face it, the kids can go to the state college, after all, we did. It did us no harm. And I don't think you'll go to jail if you agree to give evidence for the prosecution at the trial."

"You're mad, woman. The Wrights will lose everything, they'll hunt me down. I'll have a target on my back for the rest of my life."

June 1999

The trial went smoothly. Jerome had some tough questions to answer about his own ethics and the Wrights glowered at him from their defendants' chairs. He knew they would never forgive his disloyalty. But Babs sat in the gallery, watching him, supporting him, willing him on while Michael and Rosie-Lee were cared for by their grandmothers and entertained by their uncles, Jethro and Leroy in a safe house until the case concluded. Babs and Jethro were housed separately near the court, for the safety of the whole family.

The jury pronounced a unanimous guilty verdict.

Andy and his father left the court room for the final time. Andy shouted at Jerome, "I may be going to jail, but you will never be free. Hotel California."

Jerome looked up at Babs. They exchanged a shake of heads and made their way into the hall outside the court room where the Marshalls were waiting.

"Follow me," the older one said.

"Say goodbye to your old lives," said the young one. "I'll bring up the rear."

The older man glowered at him. Babs followed him out. Jerome walked behind her, she got into the car on the kerb side of the car but before she had time to wriggle across to let Jerome in, he walked around the rear of the car to open the back door. The bright yellow Lamborghini raced by. It caught his ankle as he climbed in. He yelled loudly. He felt the bones shatter. Babs heard them break.

"That's Lilian's car. I saw it at her house the first time I visited. Oh God, Jerome darling are you all right?"

"It's broken."

"You're lucky you're not dead," Babs said.

. . .

Jerome required a series of operations for the multiple fractures to his ankle. Round the clock police protection kept him safe and the move to the new house was delayed by several weeks. The children became more and more used to their new surname, Sanderson, and they had extra time to practice writing it. Michael even came up with a nick name for himself: he decided that the new friends he made would call him Sandy Sanderson. He was pleased with himself.

Rosie-Lee would be known as Rosie going forward and Babs planned to use her full first name, Barbara. The whole family had had enough of the safe house by the time Jerome was well enough to travel.

"Ready to go?" the older Marshall asked.

"More than ready," Jerome said. "Let's get out of here."

The kids cheered and followed their father out to the smaller car waiting for them. Barbara would follow with her brothers and the two grandmothers in the larger car.

The drive to the airport was as early as it was uneventful. The only reminder of Jerome's injury was his slight limp. The doctors had told him to expect that, but he was relieved that this wouldn't prevent him from doing his new job.

The Marshalls watched as the family joined the line at the desk. Jerome's mother went first, and a young family joined behind her. Barbara and Jerome went up next with the children who were extremely excited because they had never been on a plane before.

A young man travelling alone, an older couple and two women travelling together joined the line next. Only then did Barbara's mother and brothers join up.

Each group sat separately, and the children were under strict instructions not to pay any attention to their relatives. Barbara and Jerome were nervous. Could the kids do this? They behaved perfectly, even during the short lay over in Philadelphia.

When the family arrived at the end of their flight. There were three Marshalls holding signs. Mrs Sanderson for Jerome's mother, Family Sanderson for Jerome, Barbara and the kids and Barbara's mother and brothers soon noticed the Marshall waiting for them holding the sign, Martha Parker and family.

"Back in New Orleans," Jerome said.

"Yes, it's nice to be back, but life will be different going forward."

"I know love, do you wish I'd done things differently?"

"I may wish we'd never met up with Lilian and Andy again, but that's on me, not you. Maybe I'd rather you'd never taken the job with them, but what's the point? We are where we are and all the people we love have come with us."

"Thanks for hosting this family barbeque, Jerome. But really, six month's money doesn't last long, does it?" Leroy said.

"No, it doesn't. It's okay for the olds, they've been given pensions. How are you enjoying working at Bourbon Orleans Hotel? It's where we spent our honeymoon."

"It's great, I love being a chef. I go to day release classes at the culinary college, but I tell you, that kitchen is a busy place."

"How is Jethro settling in?"

"It's amazing what the Marshalls can do. They swapped his Virginia credentials over to Louisiana ones. It's fantastic, his new certificates show that he studied at Monroe in the North of the State, so he's still teaching middle school. He's got too much marking to do, or he'd be here today. He'll be moving out of Mom's to his own place, I shouldn't wonder. He's always been the saver of the family." Leroy picked up a bun from the pile. "Throw a burger in there, will you?"

Jerome went over to sit beside his mother. "How are you enjoying your new apartment, Mom?"

"It's in an extremely nice new retirement complex. It's safe, secure, and quiet. I couldn't have asked for better. Also, although there are no children who live in the complex, they are welcome to visit any time. So don't cross me off the babysitting rota."

"You should be so lucky," Jerome said.

She smiled at her son. "How is your garage going?"

"Well, it's not mine, but I work for a decent guy, Robert Brown. The pay is fair and there is plenty of work. I don't think I'll be getting laid off any time soon."

"Good to know. And are the kids settled at school?"

"Yes indeed, Sandy is top of his class and Rosie says she is, whether she is or not."

"She'll charm the world, that girl. Don't worry about her. Any chance of another hotdog, son?"

He got up and walked back to the barbeque and caught sight of Barbara inside sitting with her mother. He heard them talking.

"I'm not sure I'll ever get used to the heat and humidity here. Sorry, I'm not meant to say things like that, but I can tell you, can't I dear?"

"Yes Mom. You can say anything to me. You'll get used to it."

"How is business at the flower shop?" Martha asked her daughter.

"It's a tiny shop, but it's in a great spot right on the corner of Jackson Square. I sometimes do special arrangements for guests at The Bourbon Orleans Hotel, where Jerome and I spent out honeymoon."

"Do you ever see Leroy?"

"Rarely, his hours are even longer than mine, but he seems happy. And I hear from Jethro that he's doing his usual bit of saving up a storm, so he can get his own place sooner rather than later."

Her mother smiled. "Yes, the house they found for us does have three bedrooms, but it's small. I'd like the boys to settle so that I can move into a retirement complex like Jerome's mother has done. And you're settled here, Babs, Barbara?" She corrected herself quickly. "Oh dear, so many changes."

Rosie ran in and grabbed her grandmother by the hand. "Granny, come quickly, Daddy has made you another burger!"

Martha smiled. "So many changes, but everything that matters stayed the same."

The following morning Jerome arrived at the garage early for his shift. He was always early. It was a habit that he was known for. He had had it all his life.

He opened the door and went to put on the coffee pot. He always liked to have that ready for his boss.

He looked at the sheet that detailed all the jobs for the day and was surprised to see a yellow Lamborghini on the list. You didn't see many of them in this area and, when you did, they rarely broke down.

Jerome poured his coffee. Then he heard a car horn sounding outside, He wandered towards the street, holding his mug.

"Can I help you?" He asked before he even got to the door.

"No, you've done more than enough, you traitor. I knew I'd find you somewhere when I remembered that Babs told me you'd come to New Orleans for your honeymoon. Neither of you ever did have any imagination."

"Lillian, wait!"

Lilian didn't wait. She stepped forward and pointed the gun at his chest and fired.

Jerome dropped to the ground. She kicked him into the gutter.

"Next stop, the flower shop. I like flowers. Do you like Hotel California, Jerome?"

CATS AND DOGS

THERE ARE SO MANY WAYS THIS CHAIN OF EVENTS COULD HAVE been stopped or changed so that I would not end up in this dark place. But hindsight is 20/20 vision. Vision that's a laugh.

It was the end of yet another depressing weekend and when I got to work on Monday morning, I was not at all ready to start the day. Even my colleagues noticed, and they hardly paid me any attention.

"Eileen, you've been crying."

"No, I haven't, Joan. "

"Then why is your nose red and your mascara running down your face? Have you been dumped again?"

"No! Why would you even think that?"

"You look like that every time it happens."

"What do you mean every time? It's like I get dumped every week."

"Perhaps not every week, but certainly most weekends. Wouldn't you agree, Derek?"

"Yes. So, if you haven't been dumped, why are you crying, Eileen?" Derek said.

Anna glared at me. "Is it just your way of getting out of making the tea today?"

"Of course not. If you must know, I spent all weekend at the vet's. Not that it did any good, my cat, Mrs Slocombe died this morning at 3:22 and there was nothing I or the vet could do for her. She had kidney failure and I had to let her go to save her from any pain." Tears began rolling down my cheeks again and I was sobbing. I couldn't stop. "Poor wee Mrs Slocombe, I had had her since she was a kitten and now my best friend is gone. I feel so alone."

"And I feel so put upon because I'll have to make the tea. You should get a dog; they are more robust." I heard Anna clatter the mugs together and stomp off to the kitchen.

"Don't be like that, Anna. You know Eileen is a mess right now. Just make the tea and I'll try to get her sorted so that she can do some work today."

Joan put her arm around my shoulder. She rocked me back and forward until my sobbing had stopped.

"Eileen, you need to pull yourself together. You know there are going to be redundancies. Don't make it easy for the bosses by being so hopeless. Look, my cousin's cat had kittens a couple of months ago; why don't I see if you can have one."

"I can't just replace Mrs Slocombe! She meant the world to me."

"Seriously, Eileen, you said that about Alan, and Bob, and even Colin. If you can change your men so easily, a cat should be no problem."

"If you don't want a new cat, why not get a puppy?" Anna plonked a mug of tea onto my desk.

"I know I've been unlucky in love, but I don't want a bloody puppy! Will you two just leave me alone. Piss off, both of you." Of course, just at that point the boss marched into the office. He glowered at me. I felt my face go bright red.

"Eileen Shaw my office now," he said.

I heard Anna laugh and Joan sigh as I dragged myself through for another bollocking. I tried to explain how dreadful my weekend had been and that I had been up all night making the decision to have my cat put down. He did not look impressed. He stood up and strode from one side of the room to the other. He shouted at me, berated my excuse, and made it crystal clear but if I used bad language to my co-workers again, I would be dismissed.

So, there I was on a Monday morning with no boyfriend, no cat and in danger of losing my job. I was grateful when Joan took my arm at lunchtime and said she had an idea. She suggested we eat together in the canteen so that she could tell me all about it.

I can't pretend I was good company; I wasn't even listening to what she said. I just drank my cuppa soup and chewed my slightly stale ham sandwich and nodded.

"So that's settled, my cousin has one kitten left. He'll bring it in tomorrow after work. Bring your cat basket. And you'll give the other thing a try? I'll help you set it up." I heard her say.

"Sorry, what was that?"

"Oh, come on, Eileen, I'm not going through it all again. It's a new site, surely we can manage to get even you a couple of dates. You need to get out of yourself and look forward, woman. I'll set up a profile for you tonight. Do you have a decent picture? Or better still an indecent picture!"

I spent all evening looking for a photo that I would not mind getting passed around the office, because I knew that's what would happen. Another reason for poor little Eileen to be pitied or humiliated. However, I did remember to take the cat basket with me. Mrs Slocombe could never be replaced but the tiny kitten needed a home and with her little black ears looked every inch a Princess Leia.

When I went home that night, I was armed with the profile Joan had made for me and a tiny new companion. I poured a glass of wine, ordered a Domino's Pizza, and began to explore the new dating site while Princess Leia slept in the crook of my arm.

. . .

I have never really liked dogs, although I wouldn't be without my Alsatian, Rory, now. I have been a cat person all my life. So, at that time, as I looked at the pictures on my screen, I swiped left at all the dog lovers. It was a good feeling and made me feel powerful: at last I was getting to reject people instead of the hurtful series of rejections I had suffered.

And then I saw him. He was tall, with dark hair and the deepest chocolatey dark brown eyes I had ever seen. His smile was warm and reached all the way to his eyes, even in his photo. He was casually dressed in a fashionable shirt and light chinos. His picture was taken by the seashore looking towards the sea and he had bare feet. I don't like feet. Men's feet especially are generally ugly appendages, but even his feet were beautiful. He was sitting on a sand dune, and I could see the Bass Rock in the distance behind him. That meant he didn't live far from me. The fact he preferred dogs to cats didn't matter this time. I swiped right.

To be honest, I didn't expect him to respond. I have never been beautiful. Oh, my figure is good enough, I try to keep fit. But my hair is mousey brown, and my eyes are a funny violet colour. Also, on my civil service salary, I cannot afford to go to fancy stylists, nor do I manage to frequent beauty salons for facials, massages or to get my nails done regularly. I didn't hold out much hope of a reply.

Imagine my excitement when he swiped right too. I couldn't believe it. I did my happy dance around the living room until I was dizzy and cuddled Princess Leia tightly until she jumped down to hide under the chair.

His name was Frederick. I had never known anyone called Frederick before. Frederick, Frederick, Frederick, it was a new start for me. I could put Alan, Bob, and Colin behind me. I didn't need to think about those disastrous relationships anymore, I had Frederick now.

We started our relationship conventionally enough, if meeting on the Internet is considered to be conventional at all, now. We exchanged messages through the dating site. That's the way they liked you to do it, for your own safety and so they could charge you for the privilege.

At first, our messages were short. He told me he lived in North Berwick, and I said I was in Edinburgh. We both commented on the fact we lived quite close to each other and agreed that long-distance relationships can be difficult to maintain. He shared a house with his cousin. I lived alone in a small flat in Tollcross. He thought I was lucky to have my own space, while I envied the fact that he had company. He replied with a laughing emoji and said I had obviously never met his cousin. He went on to tell me that his home was in a quiet part of town, I told him my little flat was in a busy area. He said he knew that because his last girlfriend was a woman who worked in a bank there.

Then our messages evolved and became more personal, he told me about that girlfriend, and she dumped him just because she couldn't see him anymore. No proper excuse. I told him how Alan left me for a woman old enough to be his mother, Bob dumped me for a Spanish girl, and I discovered that Colin two-timed me throughout our relationship. It was then that I explained to Frederick because of all this, I wanted, needed, to take things slowly this time.

Frederick was so kind, so understanding and he agreed that it was no surprise that I had lost all trust in men. He said it was not a problem, we would take things at my pace. He said he knew I would be worth waiting for. He could see it in my eyes, my beautiful bright shining lilac eyes. He would wait, but he asked if we could message each other directly rather than through the dating site. This meant we could both cancel our memberships. It would be so much cheaper. He emphasised that he was certainly not interested in meeting anybody else, and he hoped that I felt the same.

Did I want to date other people? No way. Frederick was the man for me. My colleagues in the office couldn't believe my luck.

"There must be a catch, Eileen. He's way out of your league!"

"Thanks Joan."

"He's married."

"No, he's not, Anna."

"He's out of work with piles of debt."

"He's an eye specialist: a professional man, Joan."

"So, what the hell does he see in you?"

"We have a lot in common, thank you very much, Derek."

I agreed with them that he was gorgeous, definitely a nine to my six, but everything was going so well. And anyway, I felt I was due a bit of luck in the love department.

"I can't see him staying interested in a boring little mouse like you with your creepy cat for company and your 1990s fashion sense," Derek said.

I ignored him. He was twice divorced and always smelt of beer. Derek was not the Adonis of the office that he liked to think he was.

Not long after that, Frederick and I exchanged mobile numbers. He texted me several times a day and always ended his message with a kiss and a smiley face. He sent me pictures of his 'just woken up face'. It was so funny, not at all like his posed shot on the site. He sent photos of his dog lying across his legs, but his feet did not seem as pretty as I remembered. Oh well, my feet were nothing to write home about either. I sent him pictures of my cat curled up in the sun, me at my desk in the office and a selfie of me hiking in the Pentland Hills. He got worried about me hiking alone, said it could be dangerous especially if I stumbled or got lost. Nobody had ever bothered about me like that before, but Frederick really cared.

As our relationship grew, we chatted almost every evening, sometimes for hours. He laughed at my stories about what Princess Leia did and shared the antics of his dog. We were really getting to know each other, and I enjoyed having somebody to talk to when I came home from work, even if it was on the phone. On the evenings that he was out playing squash with his cousin or working late, I missed the sound of his voice.

Then one day he asked, "Do you really have violet eyes? I only ask because, thanks to coloured contact lenses anyone can have violet-coloured eyes these days. Of course, the actress, Elizabeth Taylor really did have violet eyes. The first tinted contact lenses weren't available until the 1980s, so everyone knew her eyes were real."

"Oh yes, my eyes really are that weird violet colour, Frederick. My Dad always said I had eyes like Elizabeth Taylor. My Mum just used to reply, 'if she doesn't get married that often, I'll be happy. We couldn't afford that many weddings, George.'"

Frederick laughed. "I hope you won't get married that often too. I am much too selfish to want that."

I didn't know what to say. What did he mean by that? Did he want to marry me? We hadn't even met.

Then, when he continued to speak, his voice changed and sounded professional.

"The appearance of the iris, that's the coloured ring around the eye's black pupil, depends on how much of the natural pigment, melanin, it contains. The more melanin in your iris, the darker your eyes will look. You can't choose melanin levels; they are determined by your genes.

"For example, my irises are dark brown, so my eyes have more melanin than your eyes. Elizabeth Taylor's eyes had an extremely specific, and rare, amount of melanin, and, if your eyes really are violet like hers, they are equally rare. Of course, there are various shades of light eyes: blues, greens, and grays, with many in-between. Violet may have been Taylor's typical pigmentation, it's possible to have that violet eye colour, it all depends on the amount of melanin, but I have never seen truly violet eyes."

"Well, when you see mine, you will see truly violet eyes. I don't even like them. I wish I had brown eyes like yours".

"Don't wish for that. Brown eyes are extremely common. Your colour is much rarer and more beautiful." He paused and breathed in deeply. "Would you like to facetime with me Eileen? Then I could see your pretty face and gaze into those beautiful violet eyes."

"That would be wonderful," I purred. "I can look at your handsome face and melt into those big brown eyes of yours. They are so warm and comforting, like melted chocolate."

"You are much to kind, darling. I have always preferred light coloured eyes to my common old brown ones."

Darling. He said darling. He called me darling, and the thrill of that word made me tingle all over. I gasped and grinned down the phone. I was so excited; I could hardly breathe.

"Eileen, angel, are you still there? Has the line dropped? Can you hear me?"

"Yes, Frederick, yes I can hear you. I'm sorry, Princess Leia got in the way," I lied. I couldn't tell him I'd had to catch my breath.

"Thank goodness, darling. I thought you might have had an accident. You are alright, aren't you?"

He did it again. Darling. Angel. He really cared. I flushed with excitement.

"If we were on facetime, I could see that you were alright, and I wouldn't worry. Shall we do it?"

I looked down at my old pyjamas and fluffy slippers and my heart missed a beat. I couldn't let my own dear Frederick see me looking like this.

"Maybe we could start tomorrow? I'm just in my pyjamas and I look awful tonight."

"Darling Eileen, I'm looking forward to seeing you wearing a lot less than that. But tomorrow it is. Take care my angel, till tomorrow. Goodnight."

"Goodnight, Frederick."

I hung up and lay on the couch, staring at the ceiling, replaying his words over and over in my head. He called me darling.

When I went into work the next day, Derek was standing by my desk putting a mug of tea onto my coaster.

"Good morning, Eileen. How is the great romance going?" He sneered at me as I reached up to put my coat on a hook.

"Fine thank you, Derek. Not that it's any of your business."

"Ooh charming. I should put salt in your tea to see if that sweetens you up."

I ignored his snide comment and almost danced to my desk thinking; Frederick called me darling. I had hardly slept repeating the word over and over again. His lovely warm voice echoing around my head. I knew I would not concentrate today, how could I? When Joan came into the office, she noticed right away that there was something different about me. She came over to my desk.

"Eileen, you look different this morning. You're wearing makeup and you look so pretty. Is that a new dress? I don't think I've seen it before."

I stood up and hustled Joan towards the ladies' loos. That way Derek could not come with us.

"Let me get my coat off, Eileen! For goodness sake, I only said you looked different. What's the big secret?"

I moved from foot to foot as Joan took off her jacket, glancing at me nervously and then she followed me. She looked at me curiously.

"So, what's going on Eileen?"

"You'll never believe it; Frederick called me darling!"

"Never! Did he really?"

"Yes, he did. More than once. Joan, it was so romantic. I hardly slept. I kept thinking about his warm voice, loving words, and his beautiful big brown eyes. Joan, I think I'm in love."

"Eileen, you haven't even met him!" Anna said, as she walked out of one of the cubicles. She washed her hands as she continued. "He might be a down at heel tramp or an axe murderer."

"Anna's right, Eileen. You can't be in love with a man you've never met," Joan said. "Come on, pull yourself together. We better get back to our desks and start work before Derek complains to the boss."

I followed Joan into the office. Now, I was in a bad mood. I had not slept well, and she was telling me that my feelings for a Frederick were not real. How dare she? Just because Frederick and I had not met in person didn't mean that our feelings were false. We spoke every night, we talked about everything. Nobody knew more at about me than Frederick did, and I knew everything about him. And we had so much in common, I had told him I was an only child, so was he. My parents died in a house fire. He lost both of his to cancer. I was brought up by an old auntie, his aunt and uncle brought him up with his cousin. He and his cousin are still remarkably close and shared the old family home. We both like animals, I have Princess Leia, my kitten and he has a golden Labrador a dog, Harry.

While I sat there thinking about Frederick, I didn't get much work done and I even forgot to get the teas at 10.30. Luckily, Derek was there to remind me. After that, I tried to put my office head on for the rest of the day. But as I left the office, Joan whispered to me.

"Remember, Eileen, you cannot be in love with someone you have never met. It may be infatuation or lust, or perhaps at a combination of the two, but you do not love Frederick."

She was simply wrong. Of course, Frederick and I loved each other, he called me darling.

That evening, when we were talking on the phone, I told Frederick what she had said. He was taken aback.

"What does she mean we can't love each other? What nonsense! Do you feel that way Eileen, darling? I'm sure I don't."

"No, of course not, Frederick. We know all about each other, we talk every evening. Nobody knows me better than you do."

"I feel the same way," he said. There was a pause. I looked at his handsome face on my screen. He looked a bit different from the photos on the site, but that was probably the lighting. I felt so lucky to have met him. Then he said, "I think we should meet. That way we will know for sure if we are right for one another. What do you say, my darling? May I come up to Edinburgh next weekend and take you out for dinner? I like to stay at the Waldorf Astoria at the west end of Princes Street. Do you know it? Is it easy for you to get to or should I get a taxi to pick you up?"

"Of course, I know it. That was the old Caledonian Hilton. It is very fancy and terribly expensive. Are you sure, Frederick?"

"Certainly, I am sure. I can gaze into your beautiful violet eyes and hope you will love me and that they, I mean you, will be mine."

"The Waldorf Astoria is my favourite hotel in the city. Do you like the menu at the Pompadour restaurant?"

"I don't know the menu."

"I will arrange for us to get a table overlooking the castle. It's a lovely last view of the city."

"My goodness, I have never been able to afford to eat anywhere that grand." I heard his warm laughter and I smiled nervously. "What should I wear?"

"I know that you will look lovely whatever you wear, Eileen. But perhaps you could wear a pretty red dress, that way if the waiter spills the wine, you won't need to worry."

I remember thinking that if a waiter at a hotel like the Waldorf Astoria spilled the wine, he would probably have far more to worry about than I would. However, Frederick clearly had far more experience of fine dining than I did, so I took his advice. Joan came shopping with me on Thursday evening. It was late night shopping and we had plenty of time to find a suitable dress. We went into John Lewis, but I didn't see anything I liked. I decided to go to Jenners. Joan thought it would be far or too expensive, but Frederick was taking me to dinner at the Waldorf Astoria, expensive seemed to fit the bill.

There were lots of different designers and concessions to choose from. Some of the prices were eye-wateringly high and there were not many red dresses. Then I saw one, it was perfect, and it was in my size. The red velvet sat just off my shoulders. The cut flattered my figure and even made me look petite, which I am not. It was beautiful. It was also over two hundred pounds. No way I could afford that! But Joan talked me into it.

"Come on Eileen," she said. "This is the first decent date you've had in years. You've gone out with more losers than everyone else in the office put together. Splash the cash girl and buy the pretty red dress."

When I began to argue, she shouted, "Eileen, just bloody do it. I can't bear this one to go wrong because of a few pounds and a dress."

Of course, she was right. I bought the dress. I knew it looked good on me and I felt good in it. Sooner than you can imagine, Saturday came round. I decided, that having spent so much on the dress, I might as well look the part. I made an appointment to get my hair done, my nails matched my dress, and I even got a matching bag and shoes. Even though I say so myself, I looked fabulous. I had never seen myself looking so good before and, little did I know, I would not do so again.

Frederick and I had arranged to meet in the bar. I saw him at the far end of the room. He stood up as I walked in and came towards me, with a beaming smile on his face. He was shorter than he looked in his photo and seemed older than thirty. His teeth were not so white. Gosh I was thinking such unkind thoughts. I'm no oil painting.

"Eileen, darling." His voice was the same as it was on the phone. You couldn't tell height from a photo and if I'd lost my parents as early as he had, I wouldn't have aged well either. I was ashamed of myself.

"Frederick, how lovely to see you in person."

He smiled warmly and gazed into my eyes. "They are truly violet."

"I told you that."

"Yes, you did, darling, and your dress is lovely, perfect for this evening. You look gorgeous." He took my hand and led me to our table. "I ordered champagne for us to enjoy before we go through to dinner. I hope that is not too presumptuous of me?"

"No, not at all. I've never had real champagne. It's always been Asti Spumante or Cava."

"Well, I feel like this is a cause for celebration. I get to stare at my lovely girlfriend with her beautiful violet eyes all night." He pulled out my chair and I sat down. He treated me like a real lady. It was so romantic.

His girlfriend. He thinks I'm gorgeous. A celebration. Champagne. I was drunk with delight before I'd even sipped the champagne.

We chatted about the weather, his train journey from North Berwick, the décor in the bar and the deftness with which the barman made cocktails. We linked arms across the table and sipped champagne from the glass each other held. Then the head waiter came through to tell us our dinner table was ready. Frederick and I linked arms again and followed him into the restaurant like a prince and princess. I felt like I was walking on air. We were seated by the window with a beautiful view of the castle, as he had said. The sky was clear, and the moon rose above the turrets of the historic building. I will never forget that fabulous view. The evening seemed perfect.

"Your menus, sir."

"The lady's is a guest menu?"

"Oh yes, sir."

I smiled and took the menu proffered by the waiter.

"Have anything you like, darling. This meal is entirely my treat. I want you to enjoy it."

"But Frederick, there are no prices on the menu," I whispered. "I don't want to choose something too expensive."

He smiled, the warm smile I had come to know so well as we'd facetimed. "Darling Eileen, yours is the guest menu. There are no prices so you will not feel inhibited from choosing your absolute favourite meal. Please, choose anything you like."

I smiled nervously.

The wine waiter came over to pour us another glass of champagne while Frederick led the conversation about the delicious items on the menu. A waitress brought us a bowl of olives to nibble and then a basket of breads was placed on the table. I am not keen on olives, so I picked a piece of the bread and ate that.

A different waiter came to take our order. Frederick chose the scallops followed by a rib-eye steak. I ordered the salmon mousse followed by the mushroom risotto.

"And we'll have the Chateau Ste Michelle Pinot Gris followed by the Argentinian Red Wine, the Susana Balbo Nosotros Malbec 2014 with the main course," Frederick said.

"Excellent choices, sir."

Frederick had not asked my opinion on the wine, and he ignored the waiter's comment and handed back the wine menu without looking at him.

"How do you know so much about wine?"

"My uncle was a vintner. I learned from him, and I started young." He smiled. "You see, for seafood that's higher in oil like salmon, tuna, and ocean trout you need a white wine that's richer in flavour. Chardonnay and Pinot Gris are perfect, as they have the requisite weight and power to withstand the stronger flavours of these types of fish. We are both having fish for our starters and I, personally, much prefer a pinot gris to a chardonnay. I hope you agree, darling."

"I like chardonnay. I've never tried the other one, but I'm sure it will be fine." I smiled at Frederick. He knew so much about so many things; I was beginning to feel shy. Maybe I would bore him. "Why did you choose a different wine for the main course?"

"I am having steak, and your mushroom dish has a woody, meaty undernote, so rather than a Shiraz, I chose a Malbec. The Malbec contains tannins like a Shiraz does and is said to offer a great health boost. Its flavours usually revolve around a smoky flavour combined with pepper spice and black fruits but Shiraz is best paired with game meats like duck and veal so I thought our meal would be better complimented by the Malbec, don't you agree, darling?"

"I don't often drink red wine. I did have Beaujolais Nouveau once. I didn't like it."

"I'm not surprised. It's a dreadful con the French perpetrate upon their British cousins. Ah, here comes the fish."

We ate our starters and gazed at the moon behind Edinburgh Castle. Frederick asked about Princess Leia and told me about a long walk he had had along the shore with Harry before leaving him in his cousin's care until he got home tomorrow.

My mousse was served with melba toast. It had such a delicate flavour and the wine was delicious with it. The wine waiter came to refill our glasses. I tried to decline by putting my hand over the glass. The waiter looked at Frederick and raised his eyebrows.

"Eileen darling, let him fill your glass, if you don't want any more, just don't drink it."

I blushed. "I'm sorry Frederick, I'm beginning to feel a little lightheaded."

"Don't worry darling, have another piece of bread and when your risotto gets here, you'll be fine. I must agree, I'm feeling light-headed too. I'm so excited to be here with you. Perhaps we should ask the waiter for some ice water, maybe that will cool us down. I have dreamt about this for so long, I just want everything to be perfect."

"Me too, Frederick. And it is perfect. Maybe a glass of water is exactly what I need."

A waitress cleared away the empty plates of our starters. The wine waiter brought out the red wine and Frederick tasted it before approving it. My glass was poured first. The wine was a dark red and pungent that I didn't need to raise my glass to be aware of it. I didn't like the smell at all, and wasn't sure I wanted to drink any more, but Frederick clearly enjoyed the red wine and wanted me to savour it too.

It was then that I stood up. Frederick looked at me strangely.

"I must go to the ladies' room before our main course is served," I explained.

I enjoyed my risotto and Frederick certainly tucked into his steak, heartily. He was right after all; the red wine did go well with the meal. To me, it tasted a lot better than it smelled. The waiter offered us a dessert menu when he took the plates away.

"Would you like dessert, darling?"

"You know, I think I would."

I chose the chocolate cheesecake and a cappuccino coffee. Frederick just had a double espresso.

"You'll never sleep after that," I giggled.

"I have no intention of sleeping, Eileen."

I giggled again and reached for the sugar to put some in my coffee.

"Let me help you with that," Frederick said. "Isn't the moon beautiful now?"

I looked at the dark, clear sky. "It is lovely, the view, the meal, the company, this whole evening has been wonderful, Frederick."

"I'm so glad. And I think it will only get better, Eileen."

I don't know if it happened then or whether it had happened when I went to the ladies' room, but I do know that by the time I stood up, my legs would hardly carry me. I felt very sleepy.

"I think you have had a little too much wine, Eileen."

I looked up at him and nodded. My mouth didn't work anymore.

Frederick called for the bill. I noticed he paid cash. "My fiancée has taken ill," I heard him say.

I remember wondering when I became his fiancée. Had he proposed? Had I accepted? How could I have forgotten that? Anna, Joan, and Derek would be surprised. I tried to smile but the muscles in my face wouldn't move.

"Perhaps I should take you to rest in my room, darling. Let me help you to the elevator."

I couldn't answer but I saw the waiters looking at me with disgust on their faces. I felt so ashamed but there was nothing I could do. Frederick almost carried me to be elevators and pushed the button for us to go up. But we never made it to his room because when we got in, I saw him push the button to go down to the basement. Then he stopped the lift between floors. I was confused.

He laid me down and took a teaspoon and his steak knife out of his pocket.

"You have such beautiful eyes, Eileen."

I wanted to scream. I wanted to run. I couldn't move a muscle.

I felt the knife slide into my eye socket while the teaspoon held my eye in place. I think it was then I passed out.

When I came around, the elevator was moving again. Then it stopped and I heard the doors open, but my world was dark.

A man said, "God in Heaven, Meera, another one with the eyes removed."

The woman replied, "Yes, but this one is still alive, Hunter."

HEADS YOU'RE DEAD

RUBY SWAN LAY IN THE ACCIDENT AND EMERGENCY ROOM. SHE had endured a sudden and traumatic birth. A placental abruption, which is a relatively rare but serious complication of pregnancy, had placed the well-being of both her and her baby at risk, so now two extra pints of blood and an armful of fluids flowed into Ruby to bring her back to full health. She was barely conscious, but she groaned.

Doctor Ailsa Myerscough was exhausted. Happily mother and baby survived but she hadn't delivered a baby since she had finished her training. She was grateful for the experienced team who had made for such a successful outcome because this child had not been for waiting. The mid-wife cradled the child because she had just finished all the immediate post-natal tests.

"Can I hold my baby now? Does he have all his fingers and toes?" Ruby asked.

Suddenly the door of the room was flung back and an angry woman with long, greasy blonde hair and thick black glasses stood pointing the gun upwards towards the midwife's head.

DS Jane Renwick had followed her in.

"How did she get in with that, Jane?" Ailsa asked.

"I don't know. I was waiting to drive you home when I noticed her. I tried to stop her, but she was too fast."

Ailsa nodded and returned her gaze to the intruder.

"I'll take the baby now," the woman said. She waved Ailsa aside with the gun.

Ailsa watched the midwife draw the baby closer to her chest to try to protect the boy. The doctor stood and stared at the woman. Her heart beat fast, but she spoke calmly.

"You can't take that baby, it's not yours."

"It's as much mine as it is hers."

How had this woman got into the hospital? Where had she got the gun? Would the sleepy young mum think to pull the cord for more help? Ailsa wondered if she was going to die. She glanced towards DS Jane Renwick who stood quietly beside the door. The woman couldn't leave with the child without Jane moving away from the door and Jane didn't seem to be about to do that any time soon.

"What do you mean the baby's yours? That woman has just given birth," Jane asked.

"Why can't I hold my baby? Why is that nurse holding a gun?" Ruby asked.

Jane replied decisively. "She's not a nurse, but she is holding a gun, and she wants your baby. She says it's hers."

Ruby winced as she struggled to sit up and focus on the woman.

brandishing the gun. Suddenly she opened her eyes wide.

"Oh, God, Pearl, no! You can't take my boy."

"Who is she?" Jane asked.

"Eric's mum."

"Aye you thought you'd get away with it, didn't you, Ruby? This little mite is all I've got left of my son and he's mine. You're not fit to be a mother!"

"I'm clean, Pearl! I've been clean for two years. When I got pregnant, that's why I moved away. I had to give myself a chance to stay that way. Eric wasn't strong enough he couldn't give up the smack. It had too strong a hold. That's why I left him."

"You bitch. You left him a broken man. The tears he cried for you."

"Only when he was high, Pearl. Otherwise he was working out where his next fix was coming from. Remember how he stole and fought to get his fix?"

Ailsa moved a step closer to Pearl. Maybe she could get near enough to grab the gun.

"Pearl, you broke him. With your drinking and the drugs and the thieving. Why do you think he was taken into care as a kid in the first place? He never recovered from that."

"You were in care too!" Pearl retorted.

"My parents died in a car crash. It was different. I was in care because I had nobody. It was too fucking lonely. That's how I met Eric and why I first tried heroin." Ruby looked at her scarred arms. Then she whispered. "It only took one time, and I was hooked, but not now and never again. Xander is too precious to lose."

"He is and you'll be a lovely mother," Ailsa said.

Pearl stamped her foot. "Enough!" She waved the gun. "Xander, what kind of a stupid name is that?"

"The name I gave my son."

"And you, you lanky bitch, don't come any closer, I know what you're trying to do. Stand back!" Pearl shouted at Ailsa.

Ailsa took a step back again. Someone must hear this, she thought. A quick glance at Jane showed her that the police detective had her hand in her pocket.

"And you. What are you doing there?" Pearl yelled at Jane.

"I'm just standing here wondering where you got that gun from and how many bullets are in it."

"I've got plenty bullets; don't you worry about that. You stand away from mc too," Pcarl said.

"No, I'm fine here, thanks. So your son, Eric, was it? He got taken into care. How old was he when that happened?"

"None of your fucking business, that's when."

"It's just that I was in care. I might have known him."

"He was five when he first went into the system, wasn't he, Pearl? They thought it would be temporary while you were in the clink, but when you got out you went straight back to whoring and dealing and you lost him almost right away. He'd have been twelve then. How he hated you for that. He was so angry."

"There were lots of angry boys in the children's homes. That doesn't narrow it down," Jane said.

"Give me my baby, nurse." Ruby said.

Pearl fired the gun. A bullet lodged in the wall just above Ruby's head. Everybody ducked; Ruby screamed.

"Now, we've established three things," Jane said.

"You what?"

"We've established you're not a very good shot and you have one fewer bullets than when you walked in, and you feel guilty about whatever happened to your son."

Pearl stared directly into Jane's eyes.

"I'm not feeling guilty. I just want that baby. He's my grandson and I'm not leaving here without him."

"Well, you're not leaving here with him. He's my son." Ruby yelled.

Pearl smiled. A conspiratorial smile and looked at the baby.

"I'll tell you what, I'll toss you for him. Heads you keep the baby, tales I take him away, and you never see him again."

"Don't be ridiculous," Jane said. "He's a child not a magic trick. And there's no way you're leaving here with the boy."

Pearl ignored Jane. "What do you say, Ruby? Going to risk it?"

Ailsa saw the young woman hesitate. "Ruby, no. You're still recovering from giving birth. Don't even think about it."

"You promise you'll go away?"

"If I lose, yes."

Ruby nodded. "Do it. Ailsa, will you toss the coin?"

"No, it's madness and totally unethical."

Ruby nodded at Jane. "Will you do it?"

"It's illegal."

"But will you do it?"

Jane pulled her hand out of her pocket. She nodded. "A ten pence coin okay?"

"Let me see it." Pearl crossed the room towards her and turned over the coin. "That's fine."

"Do you want to check it, Ruby?" Jane asked.

"Let's see. Fine. Now do it."

"Jane, you can't be part of this," Ailsa said.

Jane winked at her and tossed the coin so that it landed in the palm of her hand. Nobody saw the sleight of hand with which she swapped coins as she slapped the back of her hand and showed the shiny head.

"I'm sorry, Pearl. It looks like you lost."

"No. No. No." Pearl shouted. "You cheated you bitch."

"You examined the coin. How could I?"

Pearl glared at Jane. Glanced at Xander and then said to Ruby, "Look after him. He's all that's left of my boy." Pearl raised the gun and in one swift movement put the barrel into her mouth, pulled the trigger and fell to the ground.

"She died instantaneously," Ailsa said to Jane. "But how did you do that?"

Jane smiled. "A long time ago in the children's home, a boy called Eric had a crush on me. He gave me two ten pence coins. One with two heads, one with two tails. He told me, to keep them, and I'd never regret it."

VISIT TO VENICE

IT WAS MANY YEARS SINCE MARGORY AND HER HUSBAND, CECIL, had been to Venice, the floating city, but now this was the only place she wanted to be. It was the only place that Cecil wanted to be too. He told her that.

Margory had chosen to stay again at the Hotel Mercurio. It wasn't fancy, but it was central, and it was where they always stayed. When she woke that first morning, she took a shower and dressed warmly. She had done the same on that very first visit because February could be chilly, but this was the time they liked to be in Venice.

As she left the hotel, the receptionist smiled at her and asked if she wanted a map, but she declined. Margory knew exactly where she was going and how she would get there. She patted her bag to make sure she had everything with her. Then Margory noticed the receptionist's attention had turned to a young man requesting information about the city.

"A first visit?" he asked.

"Yes." The young man said softly. "Venice is a unique city; one everybody should see before they die, but not everybody gets the chance."

"I agree." The receptionist replied. "Where do you want to go today, Mr Davies? Perhaps I can suggest good ways to get about our city."

Marjory heard this as she left the hotel but didn't stop to listen to the rest of the discussion. She was on a mission and Cecil had never been a patient man, although in his professional capacity, Dr Cecil Johnstone had helped plenty of patients. She walked briskly out of the door and down the street.

Coffee and biscotti were the order of the morning. She walked along the street and across the bridge over the canal until she reached the little café where they always stopped in the mornings. She sat at the table they liked. The one in the corner by the window and saw the waiter walk towards her. He didn't recognise her. Of course he didn't, he had only been a little boy when his parents bought the coffee shop all those years ago. She and Cecil had been the first patrons. It was good to see how that little boy had grown to be such a fine man, running the cafe he had run around as a child. It made her feel good to see the next generation doing well.

"What can I get for you, this morning, lady?" he asked.

As she gave him her order, she noticed the young man she had seen at the hotel reception walk in and sit at the other window table.

He smiled at her and bid her good morning in broken Italian as he pulled out a chair and asked for a black coffee. He didn't order anything to eat. It was only then she noticed how thin he was.

When he noticed her looking at him there was a glimmer of recognition, but he clearly couldn't place her.

She said, "I think we're staying at the same hotel."

"Ah yes. Wondered where I remembered you from. Do you have a nice room?"

"It's fine. It suits my needs. I just sleep there. I want to see as much of the city as I can, while I can."

"I know what you mean, there's so much to see. And so little time." He added. "Holidays are always too short, aren't they? I'm

Ted, Ted Davies, by the way." He smiled at her. The smile shone from his eyes, and she couldn't help reciprocating.

Just then the waiter brought her breakfast and his coffee. She watched as Ted added more sugar than she thought would dissolve in the cup and stirred it slowly. He should be better eating something, rather than taking in those empty calories. She always said that to Cecil and was about to offer Ted her pearls of wisdom, but he turned his head and looked out of the window. He smiled and waved at a little boy who passed, and the child waved back. This brought their conversation to an end, but she did notice him add yet more sugar to his coffee before he drank it.

Margory sipped her coffee and stared at her wish list of places to revisit; it included nowhere she hadn't been before. That wasn't the point of this trip at all. There were many places she and Cecil visited in Venice that they wanted to visit again, so she dug into her bag to get a pen and mark up the list. She didn't notice the young man leave.

The first highlight of today was to be time at the Basilica di Santa Maria Gloriosa dei Frari, so she settled her bill, left a more than generous tip and patted her bag before leaving the café and walking along the street to join the line to wait for the vaporetto. This would take her towards San Marco. She enjoyed being back among the canals, familiar buildings and hearing Italian spoken again. She was sorry her spoken Italian wasn't better, but she understood most of what she heard and could read the language well.

At San Toma, she alighted and took a few photographs before realising there was no point. She had nobody to share them with, and she would never look at them again. A tear trickled down her cheek.

Margory brushed it away angrily and turned towards the Basilica. It was just as outstandingly beautiful as she had remembered. This building dated back to the thirteenth century, and that fact alone took her breath away. She bought her entry ticket but shunned joining any of the groups being taken around to have the art works explained to them. Cecil's medical expertise had allowed them to travel the world as he lectured at conferences. He became a fount of knowledge about art too and explained the intricacies of Venetian art to her often over the years. She didn't need a twenty-something year old art undergraduate telling her about the polyptych in the sacristy. They would have learned the history of the piece commissioned from the painter Giovanni Bellini by the three sons of Pietro Pesaro, by rote. She and Cecil knew this piece and he admired every inch of it with his soul. She felt the delight build as she stood with him to enjoy it.

Did these thoughts make her sound snobbish? Probably. She didn't care. Cecil had broken her heart and now nobody else could touch her.

Almost two hours later she left the Basilica and made her way to the Rialto Bridge. It was busy. All the little shops were bustling with tourists and the lines to wait for a ride in a gondola were longer than she had anticipated. She sighed and debated with herself whether to wait or have an early lunch.

On balance she decided the queues in the afternoon would be even longer, so she decided to wait. A gondola ride now cost almost a hundred euros: the first time she and Cecil visited the city it was only a tenth of that, and the currency had been counted in lire, not euros. Everything changed and she didn't think it had all been for the better.

Well, of course it wasn't, or they would be in that gondola or at home in Devon watching *A Move to the Country*. Oh Cecil. She began to cry soft tears again and patted her bag. The littlest child from the young family in front of her noticed. He could have been no more than four. The boy took her hand and gave it a slobbery wet kiss and said something too softly for her to hear. Still, she understood the sentiment and it helped. His mother pulled him away to keep up with those in the queue ahead of them, but he caught her eye again and smiled.

The gondola ride was a delight. As the gondolier helped her out of the boat at the end of it she spotted a little bar further down the street. She decided to stop for lunch there.

They had only been here once on their last visit before the cancer took their final hold of Cecil. His face etched with pain in sympathy as he told her about a strong dose of morphine that was administered to defeat the illness. He was such a good man. He would do anything to save his patients from suffering. They were lucky to be in his care.

She studied the menu and ordered mortadella and salad as she had the last time they sat in the trattoria. She washed it down with a large glass of chianti. She didn't normally drink at lunchtime, but in the great scheme of things, what did it matter?

As she got up to leave she saw Ted from the hotel. He looked even happier than he had in the morning. When he noticed her, his smile broadened.

"Hello, we meet again," he said. "I'm sorry, I've forgotten your name."

"Marjory." She forced a smile.

"Wasn't that café this morning a delight? I enjoyed people watching as I had my coffee. Have you had a good morning?" He asked.

"I've seen some things I wanted to see."

"Gosh, yes. There's so much to be ticked off your bucket list here, isn't there?"

"If that's meant to be funny it's not. Now, excuse me, but I must be on my way." Then she noticed the small plate of antipasto in front of him. "That won't keep you going for long,"

"It doesn't need to. I don't have much of an appetite these days." He smiled at her and started eating.

Marjory didn't think it was her place to enquire further. That would be terribly un-British, so she shrugged her shoulders, patted her bag, and started making her way towards the Guggenheim Museum.

The collection was one of her great favourites. While Cecil

always loved the traditional art, the talent displayed in more modern pieces were her own true love. He would just have to put up with it today as he always had before.

As she paid her entrance fee, she spoke to the girl behind the desk. "The first time my husband and I came here we saw a most wonderful exhibition of works by Andy Warhol."

"Oh, I don't remember it."

"I don't suppose you do. It was the summer of 1980. We were here at the same time as President Reagan and Margaret Thatcher and the rest of the G7. There was heavy security all over the city. Everywhere was busy."

"Hmm. I was born in 2004. Enjoy your visit," the girl said as she handed Margory her ticket.

Margory blushed. Why should she feel embarrassed? She patted her bag again and walked away to enjoy the present exhibits. There was so much to see.

She enjoyed the masterpieces by Magritte and Klee and spent time admiring *The Moon Woman* and *Enchanted Forest* by Jackson Pollock. However, after gazing at the works by Picasso, she came upon the paintings and drawings by Salvador Dali and remembered the visit she and Cecil made to St. Petersburg in Florida to see the impressive collection of paintings in the Dali Museum there.

They had been lucky to be able to pursue their love of art all over the world, but they always came back to Venice.

Suddenly, Margory realised how tired she was. She sat down on a bench opposite the painting by Alberto Giacometti, *Woman with her Throat Cut.* No, she couldn't do that. She sat until she felt better and decided to stop by the museum café for a coffee and a piece of cake.

She and Cecil hadn't been there before, so it was something new. Margory had no sooner begun sipping the drink and eating the overpriced, tasteless cake when she remembered why they had chosen not to eat there on all their previous visits. Nevertheless, she was older now and needed to take things more slowly. She felt better as she patted her bag and got up to leave.

On her return to the hotel, Margory went to her room and was grateful that somebody else had made her bed and cleaned the bathroom, but they had changed the towels when they really didn't need changing and she had hung them up, indicating she would happily use them again. Why did hotels do that? Why tell you how to show you don't need a change of towels but do it anyway?

She was too tired to worry about it for long. She lay down on the bed and fell asleep.

It was pitch dark when she woke, but it wasn't that late. It was February and, of course, the days were still short. Dinner would be served in the dining room downstairs and Margory didn't want to go any further. She got up, washed her face, and lifted her bag to walk downstairs and eat.

"Have you reserved a table?"

"No, I'm sorry, I haven't." Margory looked around the half empty dining room and doubted this would pose a problem. She was right. Nevertheless, she was escorted to a small tale for one just beside the door to the lavatories. "May I take that table over there instead?" She pointed to a larger table in the middle of the room.

Grudgingly the server agreed that the other table was also vacant and held Margory's chair for her before handing her a menu and a wine list.

Just then, Ted walked in. "Margory." He hailed her across the dining room and waved.

She looked up and instinctively picked up her bag from the floor and put it on the chair beside her.

The waiter and Ted spoke quietly and then Ted walked over to her table.

"Margory, if you're eating alone, may I join you? I'm on my own too and would love to have someone to talk with about this beautiful city."

She looked up at him and saw him clearly for the first time. He was thin. Too thin. And tall, well over six feet with close cropped mousey brown hair and clear intelligent grey eyes. His spectacles dominated his face because his face was pinched and gaunt. Why did he remind her of Cecil? Cecil claimed to be just under six feet tall, but if he were five feet eight inches, he was lucky. His black hair and dark brown eyes he had inherited from his Welsh mother, the self-confidence he shared with his father.

"Margory? May I sit here?"

She realised that Ted was still there and waiting for her reply.

"I'm sorry. I'm not very good company. I doubt..."

"Me neither, I did so much today that when I got back here, I fell asleep." Tim smiled his wide-open smile. "I planned to explore somewhere fun for dinner, but when I awoke just now, I was too tired." He paused. "I thought I'd just eat here because I didn't have the energy to go anywhere else. I must save myself for all the things I want to see tomorrow."

"It would be fine, but..."

"Thank you, Margory. It's much nicer to have company at dinner."

She sighed.

He pulled out the chair opposite her and sat down.

This wasn't what she meant at all, but how to tell him? He seemed to be a pleasant enough young man, but she wanted to be alone with Cecil. They would be together now and always.

They surveyed the menu in silence. Well, what was there to say? She was stuck with him now. Each ordered their meals and charged them to their respective rooms. Margory shuffled her feet, patted her bag, and moved it onto the chair on the other side of her to make room for Ted.

He sat down then the young man began to speak. "Is this a first visit to Venice for you?" He asked her.

"No, not at all, I've been here many times. But this will be my last visit." She didn't look at him as she replied. She stared at her bag.

"You are lucky to know the city well. It's my first time here.

There's so much to see. But how can you know it will be your last visit? None of us know what the future holds."

"That's where you're wrong. I know exactly what the future holds."

The waiter brought a flask of water to the table and two half carafes of wine. Red for Margory, white for Ted. A basket of bread and some olive oil for dipping quickly followed. They both reached for the same slice. Ted smiled. Margory frowned.

"So what did you see today?" Ted asked. Without waiting for her reply, he continued. "I went to the Doge's Palace. I've always wanted to see it. I got there by boat. It was wicked!" He became more and more animated as he spoke. "Can you believe it dates back to the 14th century? I mean that's the 1300s. I was amazed. Of course I've seen pictures of the outside before, but it was truly fascinating to enter that historic building. I went in through the Porta del Frumento, approached through the colonnade under the 14th century waterfront façade..."

"Yes you would. That's the public entrance."

He didn't pause for breath. "It was breath-taking just to go in. And then the art inside. What a treat. So much history to see. And to wander around St. Mark's Basilica it was an emotional experience."

"It is. I want to revisit..."

The waiter brought their meals. Margory had chosen pasta. She and Cecil did love the fresh pasta in Italy. It was nothing like that dry, chewy stuff you got at home. She noticed that Ted chose a starter again, the antipasto. It looked delicious but she didn't think it would sustain the young man well.

"What are you having for your main course?"

"Oh, I don't eat much nowadays, Margory. I don't really get hungry. You know how it is."

"Not really, no."

"So what did you see today?" he asked again. Then he went on, "Of course I saw you near the Rialto bridge at lunchtime. Wasn't it busy? I suppose a lot of people come at this time of year for the Carnival. I want to see something of that. Is that why you've come too?"

"Not really, no. It's a coincidence."

"I had coffee in St. Mark's Square today. I couldn't afford anything to eat. I'd have needed to take a mortgage to get something. And I doubt anybody will be giving me a mortgage anytime soon."

"Nor me."

"So what did you see today?"

She decided to reply quickly, before he meandered down another path. "Just went to revisit some of our favourite art works. Cecil and I always enjoy the variety of art in Venice."

"Cecil?"

"My husband."

"I don't think I've met him yet."

"No, he died last summer. Suicide."

"Suicide? How shocking! That must have been awful for you, and him. To be in such misery."

"It was tragic. He was sorely misunderstood. He couldn't bear it. So this is one last visit to Venice."

"I understand."

"I doubt it."

The waiter took their plates and Margory ordered a cappuccino while Ted requested an Americano. Margory counted as he added six sugars.

"What are your plans for tomorrow?" Ted asked.

"I'm going to the islands in the afternoon..."

"Murano, Burano and Torcello? So am I. I wonder if we're on the same tour?" Ted dug into his pocket and retrieved a battered wallet. He took out his ticket and showed it to her.

"It would seem we are."

"That's marvellous. It's been a bit lonely travelling Europe on my own without Amy."

"Amy?"

"My fiancée."

"Why didn't she come with you. Couldn't she get the time off work."

"No, it's not that. She's gone ahead, but I do miss her. It'll be nice to have your company, Margory. I'm going to do a tour of La Fenice. It's the opera house that was once the heart of Venetian high society and the golden age of Italian opera. It's been rebuilt since it burned down in 1996. I believe the architecture is amazing. That's my thing, architecture. I studied it at university, but I've never used my degree. Too much else going on, but at least I met Amy and now I've got a new friend in you."

Margory tried to smile.

"We both have busy days tomorrow. I need so much more sleep than I used to, so I'm going upstairs, but hopefully I'll see you at breakfast at the nice little café we found this morning." Ted stood and thanked the waiter before he left.

Margory watched him go and decided to order another coffee, decaf this time, just to give her time to relax and breathe alone, with Cecil, like always, just the two of them.

In the morning, Margory left the hotel a little later than before and was pleased to see nobody else in reception. She patted her bag and strode in the direction of their café, confident that she would enjoy their time alone this morning. The afternoon was going to be difficult. She hadn't planned on company and, to be honest, Ted might get in the way, but hopefully he would be too entranced by the boat ride to notice her much.

She was deep in thought as she entered the café until she heard a familiar voice.

"Good morning, Margory. Join me. Did you sleep well?"

"Not really."

"So did I, those beds are really comfortable, but I didn't need all those pillows, did you?"

The waiter took her order and Ted asked for another black coffee to drink with her.

"Please don't bother, I know you have your tour of La Fenice this morning and you've been looking forward to it, I wouldn't want you to be late on my account."

"You're so thoughtful, Margory. Don't worry, the tour doesn't start until ten. I have plenty of time, and a coffee in company will be nice."

"When will you catch up with Amy?" She asked as the waiter brought the coffees and her biscotti to the table.

"That's a nice way of putting it. I don't know exactly, but I hope to get to Athens first."

"Another wonderful city."

"You've been?"

"Many times. Art History is Cecil's great love."

"Apart from you, of course."

She nodded and bit into the biscotti. The familiar taste of the crunchy almond bread brought tears to her eyes. She wiped them away briskly with her napkin as Ted waved to a couple passing along the pavement.

"Do you know them?"

"No, not at all, but they looked rather glum. I thought a smile and a wave might improve their morning. Anyway, It can't do any harm."

"I suppose not."

"What are your plans for this morning?"

"Just a ride to St. Mark's Square and I have pre-booked a ticket to allow me to visit the Basilica. I'll take a wander around there and then go to a little place I know for lunch before our trip to the islands."

"May I join you for lunch?"

"Gosh, I don't even know the name of the trattoria, I'll just know the place when I see it." She lied badly but didn't want his company any more than she had to have it. She saw him look disappointed and she almost felt guilty. "Sorry."

"No. No worries. I'll see you on the boat." He smiled, that wide warm smile she had begun to know. "I better run, I was early, now if I'm not careful, I'll be late for La Fenice, and I don't want that." Ted left money on the table, waved to the waiter, nodded to Margory, and left.

The waiter came to pick up the money and clear Ted's cup and saucer.

"Il conto dettagliato," Margory asked for her bill. The waiter told her the amount outstanding, and she handed him the money before finishing her coffee. "It's nice to be back," she said as she walked out, patting her bag. She left the café to make her way to St. Mark's Basilica.

She stood in front of the Pala d'Oro. It was breath-taking. This had always been a favourite stop for Cecil and thoughts of him filled her head as she gazed at the Byzantine altarpiece.

"Why?" she thought. "What on earth were you thinking, dear?"

She heard an American voice rise behind her. "But Mommy, I'm so bored. Take a picture I'll look at that old stuff later. I want a cola."

Margory turned around. She couldn't help herself. She said to the parent, "Yes, do take him out of here. He's ruining the aura of the basilica for everyone else. Why waste it on such an ungrateful child?"

The mother glared at her but had no adequate response. She grabbed the child by the wrist and dragged him to a different room, chastising him loudly all the way.

When quiet resumed, Margory returned her attention to the beautiful panel in front of her. It is guarded by protective glass now after Napoleon stole some of the precious stones that adorn it back in 1797. Cecil told her the story every time they visited. She knew the date well. Still, the panel of gold embedded with hundreds of gems amazed her every time she laid eyes on it. The gems included 1,300 pearls, 300 emeralds, 300 sapphires, 400 garnets, and hundreds of amethysts, rubies, and topazes. Who could blame Napoleon for wanting to take just a few? Certainly not Cecil, he was said to have done far worse, but he was misunderstood. And can you condemn someone you love? Margory couldn't.

When she left the basilica, her eyes need time to adjust from the dark to the light. She blinked feverishly and her eyes were filled with tears. How Cecil's reputation had been damaged. The memory was too awful to bear. He should have been lauded for the ultimate care he gave his patients. She shook her head to get rid of the thoughts. She also had to get used to the Spring sunshine breaking through the clouds. Then Margory gathered her strength, patted her bag, and made her way to the little trattoria where she planned to eat. Her heart sank when she saw Ted ordering lunch.

"Margory!" he called. "What a coincidence. Did I find your restaurant by mistake? Do join me. I've just ordered, but I'm sure the waitress can take your order when you're ready and we can eat together. Did you enjoy this morning?" His wide, infectious smile almost made Margory smile back.

"Thank you, Ted. I did. Have you had a good time?" She asked politely. By now she knew that her enquiry would set Ted off on a monologue about La Fenice to which she didn't need to listen, just mutter occasional platitudes, and immerse herself in her own thoughts.

She ordered her favourite fish dish, sarde in saor. The thought of those sardine fillets marinated to a sweet and sour perfection made her mouth water.

She was so lost in thought that she forgot to pay any attention to Ted at all.

"Margory? Margory?"

"Yes, sorry. How was your morning?"

"I've just told you. I was asking after yours."

She could hear slight irritation in his voice and was glad that the waitress brought their meals. His face again broke out into the grin that was becoming so familiar.

"Thank you, this looks lovely," he said. The waitress smiled.

"You eat very small portions. That hardly looks like enough to keep you going," Margory said. Then she blushed at her bluntness. "I'm sorry, it's none of my business. Forgive me."

"What's to forgive? You are right, I don't eat big meals now. Little and often, that's my lot."

"Why is that? Of course if you don't want to say, please don't."

"I don't mind. Your sardines do smell delicious." He smiled. "Do you remember, I mentioned Amy?"

"Yes indeed. You seem very fond of her."

"I am, was, I mean. She and I were to be married. We met when we were being treated for cancer, but she went on before."

"I thought you were meeting her in Greece?"

"No. I hope to get to Greece, but Amy will never see it. She was murdered last summer. You may have read about it in the papers. Her doctor decided she had nothing left to live for and ended her life. He tried to claim it was the best treatment for her, then that it was suicide, but Amy would never kill herself. She had me. We planned to be married the following month, but he killed her. Murdered her. Slaughtered my dreams and destroyed my future.

"When they investigated, it turns out the destructive bastard murdered many more of his patients. Hundreds. Claimed they were mercy killings."

"Oh dear, Cecil." She muttered.

"Yes, that was it. Cecil Johnstone. The brute's name is etched on my soul. He committed suicide himself rather than face justice."

"Oh no, Cecil. This is too awful." She whispered.

"Too awful, indeed. Family and friends crowd funded for me to visit all the places Amy and I spoke about visiting. It was lovely of them, so I'm determined to enjoy everything for them, for Amy and for me. I suppose you're doing the same for your husband, Margory." He signalled to their waitress. "Let's have a coffee before we go on our tour of the islands." He looked at her, and they ordered their drinks. "I'm so glad we met. It's nicer to have someone to speak to rather than spending the trip on my own. Tell me about your husband. His name was Cecil wasn't it?"

What could she say? What could she tell him? She spoke quietly.

"Yes Cecil. He was very knowledgeable about art. Italian art especially. He lectured around the world, and we were able to see so many artistic treasures."

"Was that his thing? Was he an art historian?"

"Sort of."

The coffee arrived and they sipped the drinks.

Then Ted spoke. "Imagine being so arrogant, so conceited, that you think you know when someone else's life should end. Taking the decision to deprive them of any future they may have." He looked at her. "I try not to be bitter, because it's not what Amy would want and it's not how she would be, but it's really hard." He got up from his chair. "We better go, we don't want to miss the boat." He smiled.

They paid their bills and Margory patted her bag as they walked towards the gathering point.

"I'm looking forward to this, aren't you Margory?"

"In a way, I suppose I am."

They were well on their way to Murano when everybody else on the boat was straining for their first sight of the island. Phones and cameras held high to capture the view. Margory turned away from them. She took the sealed cardboard urn out of her bag and kissed it before throwing it into the Venetian Lagoon.

Ted turned around and saw her. "What are you doing, Margory? You can't just toss rubbish into the sea."

"It's not rubbish. I have carried Cecil's ashes with me for our last tour of his favourite place on earth. He was such a compassionate doctor and so misunderstood; you just didn't know him."

"Doctor? Medical doctor? Margory, what is your last name?"

"He meant well. He did. He tried to help every one of his patients and when it came to the point where he could do no more, he couldn't bear it."

Ted held her arm tight and hissed in her ear. "What is your fucking name? Was Cecil Dr Johnstone?"

"Yes, I am Margory Johnstone, and I was proud to call Dr Cecil Johnstone my husband. He was such a good man."

"A good man? He killed hundreds of people. He killed Amy before I could make her my wife. You are deluded, you stupid old woman. You should join your arrogant husband now."

"I must do just that."

"Good. Then goodbye and good riddance to you both, Margory," Ted said. He lifted her with a strength and speed he no longer thought he possessed. Then he turned towards Murano. Nobody noticed the slight sound of splashing water as Margory entered the lagoon. She didn't call for help.

It wouldn't be long until they were on the island. He would see how they made the traditional Murano glass. He would buy a glass decoration in memory of Amy. Blood red. That would be a good colour.

Assisted suicide Cecil called it.

THE PARTY

THE ROOM WAS BRIGHT AND NEWLY PAINTED A LIGHT GREEN. THE light shades were old-fashioned cream-coloured things with tassels. There were lots of chairs and tables and so many people sitting around them. They were waiting for Sylvia, eating crisps and peanuts and carrot sticks with dip. The excitement in the room was palpable. Each of the guests had made an effort to wear bright colours. They all clashed with one another. But nobody cared.

There was a band awaiting the signal to start playing. The band all wore black and looked bored. They wanted to play their music, but the lady in blue told them firmly, "Not yet. Don't spoil it."

Sylvia had had heart surgery. All the guests knew she was frail. That's why they were delighted to have this chance to greet her again on her birthday. It was such a lovely thing for her husband to do, to arrange this surprise for her; to show her how much he cared.

Excitement filled the air and the noise of chatter in the room got louder as they drank prosecco and joked about the fun evening ahead.

Then the manager came in and announced her car had just pulled up in the carpark. The whisper went around the room. "She's here. Sssh... she's here."

. . .

When she walked in on her husband's arm, everybody shouted "Surprise".

She glanced around before grabbing her chest. She gasped as she fell to the ground. She was dead before she landed on the floor; a heart attack.

Nobody noticed her husband smile at the lady in blue.

The band struck up *Happy Birthday*.

THE CORPSE IN THE CATACOMBS

I HAVE LIVED IN PLACE DENFERT-ROCHEREAU IN PARIS, FRANCE for longer than I care to admit. I grew up in the care of my grandparents after my parents' accident and I still live in the same apartment. My grandparents are long dead.

My home is comfortable and situated on the first floor of an unpretentious building in the modest street where I know most of the neighbours and all of them know me. Or at least they know one thing about me. Or think they do.

It must be almost fifty years since it happened, but the whispers and stories are wilder than they ever were. Then, people would ask me what happened. Now, they gossip, whisper, make it up or just stare at me. I would tell them what I remember if they asked me, but nobody ever does.

My cousin, Cosette had come to visit from Marseilles. That city is on the South Coast of France, and she was excited to travel north on her own to visit us in Paris.

My grandparents were delighted she was coming. Of course, they saw me every day, and loved me dearly. However, they rarely saw their other grandchildren and it was a special treat to have time with another of their precious ones. There was much excitement in the house as the day of Cosette's arrival approached. Grandmother couldn't stop smiling, even when grandfather whistled tunelessly or covered the kitchen table with soil from his window boxes.

They both wanted everything to look good when Cosette arrived.

I was excited too. Cosette and I were close in age, and I looked forward to going shopping with her in Galeries Lafayette, walking along the banks of the river Seine and drinking coffee in the little cafes around the Place du Tertre. It never occurred to me that Cosette would want to explore much closer to home.

The day arrived. Grandfather stayed home to water the window boxes and make a large pot of coffee while Grandmother, armed with her trusty walking stick, came with me to the Gare de Lyon. All the trains from Marseilles arrive there. My goodness the station was busy! Grandmother and I stood at the end of the platform until Cosette's train arrived and then we weaved, bobbed, and strained our necks until we saw her coming towards us.

"Grandmother! Elise!" she called out. She waved and started to run towards us but bumped into an elderly man. "Get out of the way, you old fool!" she said. Then my cousin tripped over the straps of her backpack and went down with a clatter onto the hard platform. I saw the old man smirk when he saw the blood that gushed from her leg and stained her dress.

"Serves you right, you disrespectful young woman," he said.

Cosette stuck her tongue out at him and then her face contorted in pain. We could see she had torn the skin on her knee.

Our grandmother tried to push past the platform guard to help her, but he would not let her get through. It was then, to our great relief, a young man in a military styled uniform went to her aid. He picked up her luggage as if it weighed nothing and threw it onto his back. Then he picked up Cosette and carried her towards us.

"I think this injured little bird is yours, ladies. May I take her to your cart?"

Grandmother looked sheepish. "We arrived by Metro and that is how we will get home. Thank you for your kindness, sir. I'll have a look at her wound and get a bandage and an aspirin for her before we make our way."

He looked slightly confused but continued to speak. "She will be fine this time. I have seen many injuries, and this is not serious, but I have no doubt it stings and there will be a bruise to her leg as well as her pride. She must learn respect before she is endangered again." He smiled, lowered Cosette gently onto a bench and deposited her bag beside us. It was only then that I noticed how grubby and dishevelled his uniform was. He looked weary as if the weight of history rested on his shoulders. I felt sorry for him. I didn't recognise his uniform, although it felt strangely familiar.

Grandmother kissed Cosette, then turned to thank the man for his help but he was gone before we could speak to him or ask his name.

"My goodness, what and entrance Cosette. Your poor leg. That wound is dirty, so we must clean it. Is it sore?"

"It is, Grandmother. Very sore."

"I'll stay with you while Elise runs to the pharmacy. Get some antiseptic and painkillers. That will allow me to clean up her leg well enough until we get home."

"Won't the antiseptic sting, grandmother?" Cosette asked.

"Indeed, it will. But that is the price you must pay for being a clumsy girl."

"And rude to that old man," I said.

Cosette began to cry. "Don't be mean to me, cousin."

"Elise, just go. Don't bicker with Cosette. Get a move on. Let's not drag this out any longer than we must," Grandmother said. She shoved a few francs into my hand, and I rushed away from them as fast as I could through the crowd to get to the pharmacy we had passed on the way to the station.

. . .

The next day, Cosette was right as rain, but she hobbled through to the living room from my bedroom that we were sharing. She wore a large cotton bandage to protect her injured knee and I noticed that she was not above complaining about the pain when dishes needed to be washed or potatoes peeled. That made me cross. Why should I have to help with all the chores while she was here drinking coffee with Grandfather, admiring his flowers in the window boxes, and sitting commenting on the intricacy of Grandmother's knitting? I had forgotten how irritating Cosette could be and thought it was probably a good thing that she lived far enough away that we did not meet too often.

However, she could be fun too. When we all sat together at lunchtime, enjoying the hearty homemade bread and soup that grandmother had prepared, my cousin turned her charm towards me. She had clearly had enough of 'the olds' as she called them.

"What shall we do this afternoon, Elise?" she asked.

"What would you like to do? We could take the metro into the city centre and go to the Louvre. It's free on Wednesdays."

Cosette pulled a face.

"Or would you prefer to see around Notre Dame? The windows are beautiful, and the atmosphere is tranquil, if it's not too busy."

My cousin wrinkled her nose in distaste.

"If you did that, you could spend time around the Bouquinistes," Grandfather suggested.

"What are they?" Cosette sounded keen.

"They are booksellers of used and antiquarian books. They have little stalls along the banks of the Seine. I could give you some money to go for coffee and a cake."

Cosette had lost interest.

"I'm not sure I could risk walking so far with my poorly knee. I wouldn't want to be a bother to Elise. Perhaps we can do that another day."

"Perhaps," I said. I had a feeling Cosette had no intentions of taking up any of the suggestions we had made. Then she surprised me.

"Before I came, I was looking at a map of Paris and all the exciting places there are to visit, and I noticed that one of the most unusual is right here in the 14th Arondissement. Could we explore the Catacombs?" she asked. "They are very close to here, aren't they?"

"Indeed, they are. But they're not safe to explore as such. Visitors must keep to the specified routes that are lit. It would be too easy to get lost, otherwise." Grandmother glanced at me, then at grandfather. "We are too busy to take you today and I think it is a bit late to get tickets anyway."

Cosette wouldn't take a hint. "My mother told me that you hold keys to the Catacombs, grandfather. "She remembers playing around there as a little girl. Please can we go? Elise and I will be careful, won't we?" She looked to me for support.

I had been into these underground ossuaries often enough with my grandfather over the years. They didn't frighten me, but I had a healthy respect for them. My grandmother was right that it was all too easy to get lost, especially if you didn't know your way around.

I did. My grandparents knew I did but we all knew that Cosette would be unlikely to do what I said if we were there alone. My grandfather tried to explain his point of view to her, again.

"The catacombs were created in ancient stone quarries. The tunnel network holds the remains of over six million people. It is not a playground," Grandfather said. "I will be happy to show you around, but not today, Cosette."

"Please Grandfather, please, please, please. I have read about them they sound so spooky and exciting. You have a key. Please let's go."

"It's true. I'm a key holder for the main entrance, I've held it for years. But there are many secret ways in. Idiot tourists trespass there all the time. You know it's consecrated ground for the burial of the dead, don't you?"

"Does it smell awful and is it really scary being in with all those dead down there?"

"No Cosette. It's not like that at all," I said. "It is a bit damp, maybe."

"And it is always cool, even in the height of summer," grandmother said. "Tell her about them, Pierre, and we'll take the girls later in the week."

Grandfather took a deep breath. "The way the catacombs began is sad. In the eighteenth century, during the Revolution, there were so many dead people that their bones were just thrown into the stone quarries under the city."

"Oh yuck," said Cosette. "That's disgusting. What about their families? How would they feel about that?"

"I doubt anyone considered that," grandmother said. "The cemeteries couldn't cope with the multitude of deaths that occurred in a short space of time, so the authorities decided they needed a better place to put the dead. The quarries were chosen but moving of the bones from cemeteries around the city into the old stone quarries was a huge job."

"It took about twelve years to complete the task." Our grandfather paused and looked at Cosette.

"And you said the remains of over six million people are down there? Gosh that's a lot! And is it true they're arranged to be creepy? I love that kind of stuff."

"The bones were laid out according to the cemeteries they came from. Most are just stacked along the corridors, but some are arranged in patterns that create crosses, skull and cross bones and so on."

"Ooh great, real-life skull and crossbones." Cosette grinned and rubbed her hands in glee. "I can't wait to see this. So much better than the Mona Lisa or the Eiffel Tower."

"Of course, in the corridors of the catacombs open to the

public, some of the bones are arranged so that they make patterns and decorations," grandmother said.

"That's true. Wasn't it done for the benefit of tourists who went to visit?" I asked.

"Yes, it was a politician, back in the early nineteenth century who suggested it," Grandfather said. "I wouldn't have liked to be amongst the quarry-men charged with that task. They had to move the bones about to make decorative features. Can you imagine it? Working underground in the dark and the damp moving bones to make patterns that look pretty. They had their work cut out for them, and no mistake."

"Ooh how fantastic! When did you say we could go?" Cosette clapped her hands with excitement.

"Today is Wednesday. Let's go Monday or Tuesday." Grandmother's suggestion seemed to me to be accepted by all of us, so Cosette and I decided to go into the city and spend the afternoon at the cathedral of Notre Dame and touring the stalls housing the books and postcards known as the bouquinistes.

It was fun to spend the afternoon with my cousin. We bickered like sisters and loved each other dearly, even when we disagreed. We chose a postcard for her to send to her parents and found a dusty old book about the history of the catacombs for only a few francs. Cosette insisted on getting this for our grandfather, although I told her that he knew so much about the catacombs, he could have written the book himself. She didn't listen.

We stopped at a little café near our the metro station near our home and treated ourselves to a coffee each and a slice of cake between us. It was too expensive to buy a piece of cake each, but it was delicious. The sponge was soft and fresh and the crème anglaise sweet as you like. The icing on top was so sugary that we pursed our lips to suck off every last bit. It was good to have Cosette's company, joke with her and have fun.

As we neared the apartment, she asked me if I knew where the secret entrances to the catacombs were. I smiled at her.

"I don't know them all," I said. "But I was down one of them in Square de l'Abbe-Migne with Grandfather only last year when a neighbour's dog disappeared there."

"The park, just over there, you mean?" she pointed from our table in the café across the road to the place I'd mentioned. "I thought that Grandfather said that was trespassing."

"Normally it would be, but this was an emergency. And anyway, grandfather is a keyholder."

"Let's go home through the park and you can show me where you had to go to rescue the dog."

We paid our bill, jumped over the fence to shouts from the waiter and I showed off to Cosette by telling her more of the story about rescuing the neighbour's dog.

By the time we got home, our grandmother had made dinner. I felt guilty that I had not been there to help, because I knew she tired easily. I set the table, put out a jug of water and arranged the chairs so there was one for Cosette. My cousin gave Grandfather the book she had bought him, and they sat and chatted more about the catacombs. I asked Cosette if she could help Grandmother bring the food to the table while I was moving chairs, but she can't have heard me, because she didn't respond and just remained deep in conversation with Grandfather.

Over dinner Cosette told us about our family in Marseilles. Her younger brother was still in high school but hoped to go to university to become an engineer. Her older brother had just finished college and had enlisted to do his national service while her little sister, who was only ten, wanted to be an astronaut. Our grandparents laughed at this last ambition, and we all joked about how far away the moon was from Marseilles compared to Paris.

It was good to hear the family news from Cosette and to learn that my aunt and uncle, though still busy at work as schoolteacher and carpenter respectively, had managed to have a holiday in Barcelona with all their children, before their oldest child joined the army.

. . .

The following morning, I was surprised that Cosette was up before me. I didn't remember her as a morning person. She wasn't in the living room either.

"Has Cosette gone downstairs to fetch the milk?" I said. I could not disguise the surprise in my voice.

"Oh goodness me, no!" Grandmother laughed.

"We haven't seen hide nor hair of her this morning, have we, Marie?" Grandfather asked.

"She must be in the bathroom. I wish she'd hurry up because I need to go to the loo."

"Elise, that is more information than I need, but she's not there. I have just finished taking a shower," Grandfather said. "Isn't she still in your room?"

"No, she's not there. That's why I asked."

I went through to my bedroom to double check, then hurried through to the bathroom because that visit could wait no longer.

When I returned to the living room my grandparents were looking solemn.

"What is the matter?" I asked.

"The key in the lock of the front door has been turned. I don't suppose you have been downstairs already?" Grandmother asked.

"No, not yet. But why don't I run down and fetch the milk, the croissants, and petit pains, then we can have breakfast? If Cosette has gone out for a walk, she won't be long, especially if she hasn't eaten. I'll have a quick look for her while I'm out."

I knew my grandparents were worried. They felt the responsibility of looking after me most heavily and I knew they would feel the same way about Cosette.

I went into the baker's shop and asked for four croissants.

"Four?" the baker's wife asked.

"Yes, my cousin is staying with us. Please may I have four petit pains also?"

"Yes, of course."

Then the baker came through. "I have been here since three o'clock this morning. Tell your grandfather I saw another damn idiot slipping down that hole into the catacombs. You know, the one where your stupid neighbour lost her dog last year."

"I'll tell him. Have they come out again?"

"How would I know? I have bread to bake and cakes to cook. I don't have time to watch over the fools intent on desecrating the burials of the dead. Pierre is the key holder, not me."

"It is almost eight o'clock now, his wife said. Tell your grandfather not to worry, whoever it was is probably back in bed sleeping off all their excitement," his wife said.

The baker's wife was always better tempered than he was. I used to joke with my grandparents that the baker got his fiery disposition from the heat of his oven. However, on this occasion I was inclined to agree with him. It was an idiot who had gone into the catacombs, and I was afraid that she was my cousin. I wondered whether I should just go into the park and have a look down the hidden entrance but decided against it. My grandparents would be worried enough without me going missing too. I ran from the baker's, picked up the milk and charged up the stairs to our apartment.

"Is Cosette back?" I asked.

"No, not yet. I'll open the window, maybe she'll smell the coffee."

I put the bread and milk on the table and went to sit beside my grandfather. I whispered in his ear what the baker had told me.

"It can't be Cosette. I didn't tell her where any of the entrances are, and they are difficult to find in the dark. She can be as headstrong as her mother, but on this occasion, it can't be her."

I felt guilt and horror well up in the pit of my stomach. Maybe Grandfather hadn't told my cousin where the secret entrances were, but I had gone one better. I had shown her.

Grandmother called us to the table, and I took my croissant and a large spoonful of apricot jam. I spread it on each piece in turn. I swigged my coffee, although it burned my throat until at last my guilt burst out of my mouth.

"I showed her. I showed her the entrance we had to use when that silly little dachshund escaped from Madame Dupont."

"God in heaven, you stupid girl. Why did you do that?" Grandfather asked "You know how impetuous she is. She has no discipline and little respect, that one."

My grandmother had not been privy to our earlier whispered conversation. "What does this mean, Pierre? What are you saying? Where is Cosette? Do you think she has gone down into the catacombs? Is that where you think she is?"

"I think that's exactly where she is, and the idiot is probably completely lost in the tunnels. Come on, Elise, we must find her before the guardian does."

"Who is the guardian, grandfather?"

"One amongst the dead. Usually, a heroic Napoleonic soldier appointed by those buried in the tunnels to look after their own and ensure they receive the appropriate respect."

Then it made sense. The soldier who had picked up Cosette when she fell in the train station wore a Napoleonic uniform. I had seen it in my history books but hadn't identified it amongst all the commotion surrounding Cosette.

"You're not going anywhere without me. Wait til I get my stout walking shoes and my stick."

"You can't go into the catacombs like that, Marie!" Grandfather shouted.

"Just watch me." Grandmother shouted back. "And don't you dare leave this apartment without me."

Grandfather fetched his keys, although we didn't need them for the entrance I had shown Cosette. He filled a bottle of water and put on a warm jacket.

"If you two are coming, you better make sure you'll not get cold."

"There's no *if* about it, Pierre. Elise get our jackets, will you?"

When we were all properly clad, we marched down the stairs and across the street to the park. We went to find Cosette.

Grandfather entered the tunnel first and helped my grandmother through the hole.

"It's ridiculous you coming down here with a stick. You should leave the search to Elise and me."

"What and leave you without a stick to wallop Cosette with? I don't think so, my dear." Then she began to shout. "Cosette! Cosette! Where are you? Answer me! You are in so much trouble when I get hold of you."

"I doubt the threat of trouble will make her want to answer you, Grandmother."

"You may be right, but it doesn't mean she's in any less trouble. Cosette! Answer me!"

"Come on, dear. There's no point in shouting, let's get a move on and find her. Follow me." Grandfather started marching along the corridor from the entrance and we followed him until he came to the first crossroads. He stopped so abruptly that grandmother and I bumped into the back of him. "Good God!" he said.

"Pierre, for goodness' sake. Remember you have a torch and I do not. Tell us when you plan to stop."

"Stop grumbling, woman. Elise has a torch too. Pay attention." He looked right and left. "Can you hear anything, Elise?"

"I think I hear a whimpering this way," I said. I pointed to the left.

"That's strange, I could swear I heard crying coming from the right," Grandfather said.

"Well, you go one way, Pierre and Elise can go the other. I'll wait here."

"In the dark, Grandmother?"

"I have a light on my phone if I need it and you can come back to me when you've had a look each way."

"Whoever finds her will shout, but are you sure about this, dear?" Grandfather asked.

"I am sure that I would like you to get a move on and find our granddaughter rather than chattering at me."

"Very well. Let's go, Elise." Grandfather's torch flickered. "No. I really don't need that," he said. He switched the torch on and off and it came back on as strong as ever. "Thank goodness." He strode off to the right and I began walking to my left.

Although I had been down the catacombs many times, that day they felt different. There was an eerie, cold draft coming from the main entrance that I had never noticed before and the tunnels disturbed me in a way they never had previously. With only the torch for light, the shadows danced around me.

I caught sight of a skull leering at me in the main beam of light while another grinned at me from beside it and it winked at me. How could a skull wink? I heard something fall. A third skull rolled along the corridor and bumped into my foot. I screamed.

"Cosette, where are you, you bitch? That wasn't funny. Come out now!"

"Elise, are you all right?" I heard my grandmother stumbling towards me in the dark.

"Stay still, Grandmother. I'm fine. I just got a fright. I think Cosette must be hiding along here. She played a trick on me."

"A trick? I'll show you a trick Cosette. Come out now or I'll beat you even harder."

But I didn't see Cosette. Grandmother and I heard nothing else. "I must be mistaken, she isn't here. We made our way back to the crossroads and my grandfather was already there.

"No luck that way either?"

"No, but a skull rolled along the pathway. I got a fright."

"I'm not surprised. The piles of bones are much less secure in the back tunnels than in the wider ones that the tourists traipse along. Come on. I want to find that wretched girl before the main routes open."

We walked carefully along to the next junction. A pile of bones had slipped, and they blocked the left exit.

"Well, she didn't go that way. You stay with your grandmother, and I will have a look this way." Grandfather waved his torch again. It flickered before the beam steadied.

"Take my torch, Grandfather."

"Maybe I will. Thank you."

I watched him tramp along the path. I thought about how old he looked. His shoulders were bent, and he had begun to shuffle. His step was no longer the confident gait I was used to seeing. It seemed to me that he aged with every stride as he walked away.

"Look at him! He's worried sick," grandmother said. "Your aunt warned me that Cosette was headstrong. They are having such a problem with her, but this is beyond anything that I had expected."

"Grandfather must have turned a corner. I can't see his torch anymore."

"Oh dear. Will he be all right?"

"Of course. Grandfather has a map of these tunnels in his head. He'll be fine. He's probably just heard Cosette and gone to get her to lead her back."

"You're right. Go and help him. I'll wait for you here but I'm getting tired standing. Do you think it would be too awful if I sat on that pile of bones?"

"Who's going to know? Sit if you need to. I'll find Grandfather and be back as soon as I can." I looked at the concern etched on her face. "Don't worry, we'll find her. She's just being and arse."

"Mind your language, Elise. Now, go to help your grandfather find your impossible cousin."

I watched her sit heavily on the pile of bones. They shifted under her weight and as I turned to walk away, there were a couple of sharp cracks as bones below her broke and I'm sure I heard someone say 'ouch' and another voice say, 'not again'. It was spooky and I ran down the corridor that my grandfather had followed. I prayed that his torch didn't fail me. The bones piled up on either side frightened me in a way that they had never done before. I wanted to find Cosette and get out.

At the end of the corridor there was a choice of turning right or left or going straight ahead. I stood and looked for a glimmer of light. The only spark was from the right. I shouted out.

"Grandfather! Cosette! Where are you?"

I heard a loud sob.

"Elise, Elise, this way. She's here." Grandfather's voice sounded muffled. "Come this way. Help me."

I was going to speed towards him, but suddenly was aware of a presence behind me. I turned around and saw the soldier who had helped Cosette in the train station.

"Thank goodness you're here," I said. "My cousin is lost in here and I need to get to my grandfather and help him get her out. Would you assist us?"

He looked at me solemnly. "She is not lost. She has no respect; she had none in the station for the living and she has none for the dead here. Do you know that woman invaded the tomb and grabbed my brother's leg? She used his bone as a stick to poke at others. She treated us all with contempt. She laughed and joked about the dead here.

"Your grandfather has tended the tunnels for years and always treated us with courtesy and civility. You too trod the paths of the catacombs with reverence, but that woman does not and then an old woman broke my comrade's bones when she sat on them. How dare she violate these graves?"

He was furious and began to shake,

"My grandmother didn't mean to cause any harm. She is old and tired. That's all."

"What is she doing clambering in here?"

"Anyway, how can your brother be one of the people whose bones are incarcerated here if you are alive?"

"Alive? I have been elected as the current guardian of these tombs."

"But you were at the train station?"

"Yes, to meet that woman and warn her to be more respectful before she visited the catacombs. We had been warned. I failed. I let down the dead. I must be replaced as guardian by one who will succeed, be effective, protect those who are buried here."

With that he was gone. His uniform vanished and his bones melded into the patterns at the sides of the corridor. A cold shiver ran through my body, the torch flickered, and the light went out. Then I heard another shout.

"Elise, are you coming? Help me, Elise."

"Grandfather, I'm sorry, I'm coming." I ran towards my grandfather's voice, tripping and stumbling in the dark along the way. He shone his torch towards me and flashed the light in my eyes and I lurched to the left then stopped abruptly to regain my balance.

"I'm sorry, Elise. I didn't mean to blind you. Has the other torch failed completely?"

"Yes. Where is Cosette? How can I help?"

"She's here, my dear, but we can't help her." My grandfather was kneeling beside Cosette. She was still, deathly still, and quieter than I have ever heard anyone ever be. "Look. Just look at our dear girl. Our dear, dead girl."

"Are you sure she's dead? She can't be dead, Grandfather."

"She's not breathing and there's no pulse. What would you call it?"

"Oh God, what do we do?" I wondered if I should tell Grandfather about the conversation that I had with the soldier, but he was so distressed that I decided against it. After all, it couldn't be real. My fear must have made me imagine it all."

"We must leave her and phone the police. However will your poor grandmother react? I can't bear the thought of the misery this will cause her."

"Come on. Let's get back to her. She's alone in the dark."

Grandfather stood up and took my hand. He led me slowly along the corridor. We paused at the junction and then turned left, shuffling in the dim light of the one remaining torch towards my grandmother. I could hear my grandfather stifling sobs and, occasionally he dropped my hand to pull a large handkerchief out of his pocket and blow his nose.

When we got back to my grandmother she was slumped forward. The bones she had broken lay in front of her.

Grandfather shone the torch onto my grandmother and then caught sight of the bones.

"What happened here? Is she sitting on the remains of the dead? What was she thinking? The guardian will take his revenge. We must get her out of here. Out of here now, before it is too late. Marie, get up and follow me." He grabbed her hand. "Oh God! How cold she is."

"Is she dead too?"

My grandfather held her wrist. "Not yet. The guardian must have changed, and they have not yet managed to drain the life out of her. We must hurry." He looked at me with terror in his eyes. "Elise, take the torch and guide us out. I will support your grandmother."

I do not remember much of the journey through the secret passages to the park. Back outside, my phone had signal and we called the police and the ambulance. The authorities, in turn, contacted the director of the museums of Paris about Cosette's death. He had ultimate responsibility for the tunnels.

Entry to the catacombs is much more tightly controlled now than it was back then.

Grandmother was taken to hospital. She never fully recovered, but whenever she spoke it was to apologise for desecrating the graves of the dead soldiers and the pain she caused when she broke their legs. When she died, we buried her beside Cosette. Grandfather said they would be company for one another.

Grandfather gave up his keys and his responsibilities for the tunnels. We lived together for almost twenty years. We always tried to warn people not to enter the catacombs without permission, but still tourists and locals alike ignored what we told them and laughed at us behind our backs.

He was nearly ninety when he passed away. I will never forget his last words, "Elise, respect the guardian."

MY FATHER'S GARDEN

=

My father used to make me laugh. His garden was always the neatest in the village. One day, he got elephant dung delivered from the zoo. My mother complained endlessly about the stench, but his roses were beautiful that year.

He always grew vegetables too, and we ate in season. Lettuce, tomatoes, and courgettes in the summer made for back breaking work as we harvested his crop and took it into my mother, but she always complained.

The lettuces had been eaten by slugs, the tomatoes weren't red enough, and the courgettes were too big.

Potatoes, onions, and turnips were gathered in the autumn and there was more work for the family, but again nothing was ever good enough for mother.

The potatoes were too small, there weren't enough onions but there were far too many turnips. Every year it was the same; mother always complained.

When the cherries and apples ripened and had to be picked. As children, we learned quickly which fruit to pick and which to leave for another day. Mother grumbled if we got it wrong.

Father always planted his first crops in the spring. This year he had not long finished when mother became furious that he planted broad beans instead of peas. I had never seen her so angry, but father laughed about it. Mother didn't find it funny.

She murdered him in his lettuce patch. His body is rotting with the vegetables.

Mother was hanged, but for Father, I don't think there is anywhere he would rather be.

THE FALL

“We’ve got tomorrow off; shall we climb to the top of Arthur’s Seat and wash our faces in the dew to make ourselves beautiful?” Jane asked Rachael with a smile.

“I’m quite beautiful enough. You go.”

“Oh thanks a lot! Come on, a morning walk on a lovely Spring morning will be nice.”

“You have to be there by sunrise, for it to work. I’m not a morning person at the best of times. You go if you want to Janey.”

“You are hopeless, Rache, it’d be no fun on my own. Do come!”

“Where did this mad idea come from anyway? It’s just craziness.”

“No it’s not! It’s romantic and it dates back centuries.”

“Just because people have been idiots for a long time doesn’t suddenly make this a good idea.”

“Rachael, think about it. The custom is related to the Druid festival of Beltane. See, in the paper here it says there’s to be a pagan ritual and a Christina service of thanksgiving. It sounds fun. But we must be at the top of the hill by 5am. That’s when it all kicks off.”

"It sounds early, not so sure about fun, but if it means so much to you we'll go. Just this once. I'm not making a habit of it."

"Thanks honey. I agree this will be a once only event unless you enjoy it."

"Don't count on that." Rachael frowned. Then Jane started to tickle her, and they both burst out laughing.

Simon smiled at Holly. They had found the Gothic pub, Frankenstein's, near their Air B&B. It was busy, but they found a table and Simon helped Holly take off her bright red jacket.

"You look really pretty in this coat," he said.

"Thank you. It's warm and comfortable."

"And it's so bright, I won't lose you."

"Would you want to?" She giggled and soon they were enjoying the atmosphere of the pub and were included in the chat with the group at the table next to them. Suddenly the loudest lad, Duncan, slapped the table and shouted, "Tomorrow's Mayday!"

"Yeh, so what? It's not a public holiday or anything, is it?" Simon asked with a chuckle.

"No, it's better than that. There's a tradition of climbing to the top of Arthur's Seat and washing your face in the first morning dew. Isn't that right, Ellen?" Duncan said.

"Aye, to make you beautiful! I'm up for it. You coming?" She asked Simon and Holly.

"What's Arthur's Seat? It sounds like an old man's chair!" Holly laughed.

"You English, what are you like? It's the big hill, an extinct volcano really, in the middle of Holyrood Park over to the East of the city, you must have seen it," Ellen said.

"Not so much anti-English talk, we're from Dorset. What do you know about that?" Simon grinned.

"Jurassic Coast, Bournemouth and the white chalk man with a big willy!" Duncan laughed. He made a rude gesture.

"Ha ha, that's not all there is, you know. But okay, this sounds fun. How do we get to the park?" Simon asked. He didn't notice Holly frowning.

"Why don't you get a round of drinks in and we'll talk about it?" Duncan asked.

"Will do, if you order us all some pizzas," Simon said to Duncan.

The girls stayed at the table and chatted with the others in the group. Ellen explained that one of the men, Stuart, had a room in a flat near Holyrood Park and suggested they all crash there to be ready to greet the dawn at the top of Arthur's Seat.

"Is it a difficult climb to the top?" Holly asked Ellen.

"No, not too bad. Just keep to the path and don't wander towards the Salisbury Crags; there's a steep drop from the top of them. People die falling from there."

Holly shuddered. "I just wish Simon would ask me about things like this before it's a done deal. Sometimes I feel he takes me for granted." Holly paused. "Sorry, don't mind me. It's our last night, and I hoped we'd spend it alone together." Holly went on to tell them that she and Simon were celebrating their first wedding anniversary on their trip to Edinburgh. They were saving for a deposit to buy a house and had taken out a life policy in anticipation of their purchase.

"I thought you did it the other way round? You know, get the house first and the life policy to match the mortgage, don't you?" Ellen asked.

"Well, Simon thought, as it takes so long to save up for a deposit, we'd best get the policy while we're as young as we can be and get a better price on the policy."

"Makes sense, I suppose," Ellen said. "How much do you get if he pops his clogs?"

"What on earth do you mean?"

"Sorry, just a bad joke. Ooh here comes the beer. Where's the pizzas Dunc?"

"Give me a fuckin' chance, girl. I've just ordered them. Now they've got to cook them. Pass us a beer, Simon."

Four o'clock in the morning and a shrill alarm rang around the flat. Stuart's flatmates complained and were clearly underwhelmed, first by the intrusion of drunken revellers who had invaded their living room with a view to an early start and also by the booming alarm that sounded three hours before they had to get up for work and college respectively.

Simon and Holly were quiet. She hardly looked at him, although they shared a mug of coffee as there weren't enough mugs to go around and then the whole group, still drunk from the night before, left the flat and traipsed down the stone stairs as quietly as they could with the unending instruction of "Ssssh" soundly so loudly up and down the close they woke every neighbour in the block.

"This is a truly rubbish idea, Janey. Why are we doing this?" Rachael grumbled as she stumbled out of bed.

"If you'd had a quick shower, you'd feel better."

"I would not! I'd have had to get up ten minutes earlier."

"I've made you a mug of tea, I thought peppermint might be refreshing." Jane smiled.

"Another two hours of sleep is what would have been refreshing." Rachael grumbled.

Jane stood in the doorway watching Rachael get dressed. "Wear your thick socks."

"And my walking boots. I do know, Janey. I just don't like getting up in the middle of the night."

"I think I got that. Okay, this is a one off. I promise."

Rachael stood up, fully kitted out for the walk. "Good." She kissed Jane swiftly on the lips. "Now, who mentioned peppermint tea?"

Jane parked the car in the car park near the bottom of Arthur's Seat. She waited while Rachael got her water bottle and gloves out.

"It's a beautiful morning, isn't it?"

"It'll be nicer in three hours' time."

"Stop bitching, Rachael." Jane smiled. "You know Arthur's Seat is an amazing feature to have in the middle of a city. Even Robert Louis Stevenson wrote about it."

"Who?"

"You know, he wrote Dr Jekyll and Mr Hyde."

"Sorry, Janey, I didn't hear you properly. I had my head in the car."

"No problem, love. Arthur's Seat and the rest of the hills cover so much of Holyrood Park, don't they?"

"They do. And did Robert Louis Stevenson mention how many spouses had come to a sad end getting pushed off the Crags because they got their better halves up at silly o'clock on May Day morning to wash their already clean faces in the morning dew?"

"No he didn't. Now, come on you old grouch, let's get climbing or we'll be late. Look! Another group has overtaken us."

"Not so much of the old!" Rachael closed the car door and Jane locked it before they jogged over to catch up with the group just ahead of them.

"You girls coming to the top of the hill to wash in the dew?" Duncan asked Jane.

"Yes. Just a bit of fun." She replied.

"You don't need to – you're well bonny," he said.

"Dunc, you with me or what?" Ellen grabbed his arm.

"What?" Duncan asked. Ellen slapped him. "You're too easy to wind up Ellen," he said. "Race you to the top, girls." He called to Jane and Rachael.

"Oh no, not me," Rachael said. But she knew Jane couldn't resist a challenge.

"You've got no chance, boy," Jane said. She extended the length of her stride and began to run easily up the hill. Duncan had no chance at all.

Rachael walked steadily up the hill behind Jane. She found herself step by step with a young English couple and got chatting to them. Simon seemed nice and told her proudly they were celebrating their first wedding anniversary. Holly didn't say much but kept a tight hold of Simon's arm in a proprietorial way. She didn't seem to want Rachael's company and seemed cross that Simon was willing to strike up a friendly conversation.

Holly pulled Simon off the path and over to the right a bit. Rachael didn't follow them, nor did she bother to tell them that she and Jane had been in a Civil Partnership for over two years. It would seem like boasting and it was none of their business.

Holly seemed to want to be alone with Simon and Rachael could understand that, so she made her excuses and sped up a little to make a distance between them and to try to catch Jane.

"See you at the top, Rache," Simon said.

As Rachael walked ahead, she thought she heard Holly arguing and shouting at Simon. She clearly thought he had been overly friendly with her and it seemed like this wasn't the first time she had felt ignored. If only Holly knew the truth; Simon was not her type at all.

When Rachael got to the top of Arthur's Seat, Jane was already there, shaking hands with Duncan who took it in good part that he had been beaten to the top of the hill by a lassie. Ellen did not look so pleased.

"Rache, darling, to the winner the spoils!" Jane pulled Rachael towards her for a long loving kiss.

"Well done, Janey," Rachael said.

"What? Are you two a couple or what?" Ellen asked.

"For years. I can't get rid of her." Rachael smiled. She took a swig of her water then offered the bottle to Jane. "Yep, don't know what I'd do without her."

Ellen laughed and relaxed. "Well done, Jane. Congratulations, lass."

Duncan pulled out his hip flask. "Want a sip?" he asked Ellen.

She took a drink of the whisky and then offered it around the group. "Where are Simon and Holly?"

"The English couple? Are they with you?" Rachael asked.

"Aye we met up last night."

"I spoke to them on the climb to the top, but they looked like they wanted to be alone, so I walked ahead."

"It's their anniversary. They'll be here soon," Ellen said. "Now, to do what we came here for, Duncan, Stuart, all of you, get washing those faces. We can only have beautiful people leaving the top of the hill this morning."

The group all began to bend down and gather dew on their hands. They rubbed their faces and then began fooling around rubbing each other's faces. Jane and Rachael joined in.

"Are you having fun?" Jane whispered.

Rachael nodded. "I'm with you, my love. Of course I'm having fun." She kissed Jane and they laughed together.

Jane and Rachael stood with the group to watch the druid ceremony that took place on the top of the hill. A group of enthusiastic Christian worshipers were there too, but Jane noticed that they waited respectfully for the pagan ceremony to finish before shaking hands with them. Both religions wandered amongst each other, and she heard a murmur of 'Peace be with you' from the Christians while they mingled before beginning their own short service.

As the sun broke over the city, she smiled at Rachael. "Well, what do you think?"

"That was truly lovely. It just shows that different beliefs can live on the earth in peace."

"I wouldn't take two small groups at the top of a hill in the early hours of the morning to extrapolate such a profound theory, Rache."

"No you're probably right, maybe they were just too sleepy to argue." Rachael grinned and then turned to Ellen. "We're going to get off now, but when you catch up with Simon and Holly do give them my best wishes for the rest of their vacation."

"Will do. I wonder where they are. I thought they were right behind us as we trudged up the path, but I don't see them at all now."

"Right, Ellen, we've got to get down. I've got work today," Duncan said.

"Yeh, and I've got to tidy up your mess in my flat before I go to work," Stuart said. He glared around the group and a few of the others in the group offered to help, he immediately accepted. "Look! Is that Holly? It looks like her red jacket. What's she doing over there? Did she and Simon miss the path to the top of Arthur's Seat?"

Duncan looked over in the direction he was pointing. "It does look like Holly, but I don't see Simon. Do you, Ellen?"

"No, but they're awfully near the top of the Crags," Rachael said. "I did notice them veering off in that direction when I left them, and Holly didn't seem so happy with Simon."

"Hmm, she's a bit moody. She was grumpy with him yesterday for wanting them to come with us this morning. She had other plans for last night." Ellen started making kissing noises and crossed her arms in front of her to rub her hands up and down her own back.

Jane couldn't help laughing. "Let's go over and check there's no problem before we go back to the car, Rache."

"They're grownups, Janey. They're not our responsibility."

"True, but we're cops, and you know what DI Hunter Wilson says, 'Never off duty'."

"You're fuckin' pigs? You didn't tell us that before we raced up the hill." Duncan exclaimed. "Next you'll be telling me you go running for fun."

"Guilty as charged."

"Fucks sake."

"You didn't ask." Jane laughed. "Come on, let's see what's happening over there."

Jane started to jog towards the person in the red jacket. Rachael followed her and, after a brief discussion, she heard the rest of the group running behind her.

It was no surprise to anyone now that Jane reached the top of Salisbury Crags first, but as Rachael approached, she saw the person wearing the red jacket wasn't Holly. The woman wearing that coat was of Asian heritage and had a little Jack Russel dog jumping about at her feet. The Holly she had met was white with no dog.

Rachael ran faster. Jane was on her phone. The woman in the red coat was crying.

"What's happened?" Duncan asked. As he arrived at the scene.

"I don't know, Jane's just calling it in." Rachael peered over the front of the Crags, determined not to get to close to the edge.

"Watch out!" Duncan shouted. "The grass is still really slippery."

"Oh my God! They're down there. Simon and Holly are at the bottom of the cliff."

"Are they dead?" Ellen asked.

"I doubt Simon survived that head injury. He smashed his skull like an egg. Look at the blood," Duncan said. Then he spewed all over the grass. Some of the bile hit Rachael's shoe. "Sorry, lass."

Rachael shook her head in acceptance of his apology. She watched Jane draw her conversation to a close. And put her phone into her pocket.

"What happened, Jane?"

"I don't know, Rache. This lady, Mrs Kaur, Husna Kaur, was walking her dog and was about twenty feet away from Simon and

Holly." Jane turned to Mrs Kaur. "We'll need to take a formal statement from you, but could you tell me what you saw?" Jane pulled a packet of paper tissues out of her pocket and handed one to the witness.

"I'll liaise with the emergency services when they arrive," Rachael said. She saw her wife nod in agreement. "There's nothing you could have done from twenty feet away Mrs Kaur. I know it was a horrible thing to see but try not to worry." She reassured the shocked woman.

Jane led Mrs Kaur away from the group that had gathered at the top of the Crags. They stood together near the cliff top, and she saw each person in turn peek over the edge of the cliffs and retreat again ashen faced.

Holly's limbs were in an unnatural position, and she wasn't moving. Simon's shattered skull had blood and brain matter oozing from it. Jane thought it unlikely that either of them had survived. She felt bilious thinking about it.

Then she turned her attention back to the distressed witness. It was better than thinking about the death of a young couple who should be starting out on their lives together.

"What did you see Mrs Kaur?"

"Well, I heard them first. I don't usually come this far over, but Jackie, my dog, saw a rabbit and chased it. He was on the lead but it's one of these extending leads, you know?"

Jane nodded.

"That's when I heard them first."

"What were they saying?"

"I wasn't close enough to hear, but the woman was shouting at the man. His voice was not so loud, but firm. They were both angry."

"Okay. What next?"

"When I got closer I heard her say, something about 'why did they need a life policy now when they didn't even have a house. Was he planning to do her in. Was that why he never paid her attention...' "

Jane nodded encouragingly.

"Then Jackie was right beside them and her face was red and cross. She was screaming at him. She said 'well, two can play at that game'." Mrs Kaur began to cry again. "He was holding the sleeve of her jacket, like this." The woman held Jane's arm. "He seemed to be trying to calm her down. Then she got behind him and shoved him, but he didn't let her go and they both screamed as they fell. It was horrible. I saw it happen and I didn't stop it. I couldn't, I wasn't close enough."

Jane looked into Mrs Kaur's sad eyes. "This is not your fault, Mrs Kaur. You couldn't possibly have stopped it. If you had tried the momentum of their bodies would just have pulled you over too." She looked down to get another paper tissue put of her pocket.

Then it happened. There was nothing she could do to stop the fall. Jackie reacted so fast to the rabbit bounding towards the edge of the Crags. He wound the lead around Mrs Kaur's legs and jumped after the quick creature. The rabbit veered away from the edge, but the dog was not so nimble. He fell howling to the rocks hundreds of feet below. His owner followed. Her legs bound together by the expanding lead.

Jane looked in horror as she saw the look of terror in Mrs Kaur's eyes. The woman screamed. Jane tried to catch her, but it was all too fast.

The emergency services arrived and found three bodies at the bottom of the cliff. Mrs Kaur and Simon both left the scene by private ambulance to go to the morgue for post-mortems on their bodies. The paramedics took Holly to hospital, where the police formally charged her with Simon's murder before she died of her injuries.

Jane agreed with Rachael that their walk to the top of Arthur's Seat on May Day morning was a one off, never to be repeated, event.

THE SECOND CHANCE

ABBIE WALKED OUT OF HMP CORNTONVALE CARRYING A CLEAR, plastic bag containing her belongings. She didn't look back.

Her stuff didn't amount to much after three years behind bars: a few clothes that those staying behind had let her keep, a bright red mug with 'Nescafe' stamped on it, and her diaries which reminded her how much she wanted to stay out of trouble in the future.

She crossed the road and went to stand at the bus stop. The bag marked her out as a newly released prisoner, and she blushed when the old woman in front of her looked at her with a sneer before turning to look in the direction the bus would come from. Abbie just looked away.

In her pocket, Abbie held her travel voucher tight. It would get her back to Gran's flat in the Wester Hailes district of Edinburgh and then she would reunite with her family. Her gran, Barbara MacLeod, had done so much for her and her younger brother, Lewis, since their parents had died. She gave them a home, fed them, got them to school and even made them do their homework. It wasn't her fault Abbie had got in with the wrong crowd and gone off the rails. Being honest with herself, Abbie knew that if she hadn't met Josh Bryden and been so keen to impress him, she wouldn't have joined his gang, had his baby, or ended up in prison. It certainly wasn't anything Gran did wrong. She had even looked after her baby, Daisy, when she grew too old to stay with Abbie in prison.

She was glad that at least Lewis was a good boy and made Gran proud. She hugged herself tight at the thought of holding Daisy, hugging Gran, and teasing Lewis.

Abbie smiled and counted her discharge grant again. Seventy-nine pounds, the last time she had that much money was when she helped Josh break into that old woman's flat.

Nobody was meant to get hurt. They went to steal her antiques and money. Josh told her they had to be careful only to take the real stuff, not replicas or silver plate. They made more noise than usual getting in and rummaging about her home turning things over to check the marks. Josh knew about antiques. Of course, the old woman heard them and challenged them.

Abbie was holding a delft figurine tightly; Josh would give her a bollocking if she dropped it. The old woman shouted and waved her stick at them. She hit Abbie's arm. It snapped like a twig. That old bird gave it with some force.

Abbie yelled and cradled her damaged limb but didn't let go of the old bat's ornament.

If only the old woman had let them out, but she was determined and when she lunged at them again, Josh stepped in front of Abbie and shoved woman. Oh God, it still made Abbie's blood run cold inside her to think of the old woman stumbling, calling out for Jesus before she fell backwards and split her head on the fireplace. The stick fell from her hand and blood dribbled out of her ear.

Josh felt her neck. "Fuck! She's dead. We've got to get out!" He shouted. He pulled Abbie's broken arm; she fainted and collapsed in pain.

"Come on idiot!" Josh grabbed the ornament from her and she saw him take the woman's keys and purse and then he yelled at her again, but she couldn't move. The pain was unbearable. "Sod this,

I'm outta here – but don't you dare open your mouth, or you'll be sorry."

She woke to the sound of the police battering at the door.

She didn't open her mouth. Although he left her to take the blame, to find out she was carrying his baby, and to spend three years of her life rotting in Corntonvale for the crime that was his idea, his plan, and his reward because he never got caught. But he was right about one thing – she was an idiot. She should never have got involved with him in the first place.

It was easy to be wise now. She wouldn't go down that road again. In the three years she had been inside, Abbie had learned to cook and bake, and Gran had spoken to her friend, Laura, who ran a wee sandwich place. She would give Abbie a trial and if it worked out, Abbie would get a job in the shop. Gran was always looking out for her.

Abbie had been working for Laura for three days when Josh strolled into the shop and smiled.

"Well, if it isn't my own little idiot. How you doing Abbie? I'll take a bacon and egg roll and a cola. Oh and throw in a big bag of crisps and one of those packs of biscuits for the lads."

Abbie put the biscuits and the cola on the counter while she turned to make his roll, but Laura came bustling through from the back shop as soon as she heard them speaking. "What are you doing in here?" She waved her hand at Josh. "I told you; you're barred!"

Josh laughed at her, grabbed the juice and biscuits, and ran away.

"That one is bad news," Laura shook her head. "You never put anything on the counter until you've got their money."

"Oh Laura, I'm sorry. I didn't think. Take it out of my wages," Abbie said. She started to cry.

"Come on, love, it's not that bad. It's only a packet of biscuits. It's not worth crying about." Laura hugged Abbie until she calmed down. "Now you go and make us a nice cup of tea and I'll serve these good folk to finish the breakfast rush. Laura looked at the queue building up and started serving.

Abbie nodded and went through to the back shop to make the tea.

It wasn't long before Gran stopped by with Daisy. "We're on the way to the play park," she said. "But Daisy wanted to see Mummy at work, so we thought we'd come this way. Can she go through the back with Abbie for a few minutes if you're quiet, Laura?"

Laura agreed that would be fine and Abbie held out her hand to help Daisy toddle through with her.

Gran and Laura chatted quietly, and Daisy sat on a chair sucking on a chocolate finger while Abbie spoke gently to her and made three cups of tea. Gran was always ready for a cuppa.

Suddenly the back door of the shop flew open. Josh lifted Daisy off the chair. "I thought it was your Gran I saw. I followed her all the way here. The old bitch hasn't let me see my child once since Daisy's been with her. Now it's my turn, Abbie." He ran towards a waiting van.

Abbie screamed. "Daisy!"

Daisy dropped her chocolate finger and started to cry.

"Daisy!" Abbie ran towards the van, but it was already driving away.

Gran and Laura rushed back through to the back shop towards Abbie. They looked at Abbie in dismay.

"Where's Daisy?" Gran asked.

"Josh has taken her. He made off with her in a van. Oh Gran, I'm such an idiot. I can't do anything right."

"Don't you dare say that. You gave birth to that wee flower and you're a good girl. That Josh is the problem, but he could charm the birds out of the trees that one."

"You're a hard worker here, lass. We'll sort it. We'll get her back."

"How?"

"My brother's a policeman. He'll help."

DI Hunter Wilson was on his way out of the station when a phone rang. It wasn't the official line, so he stopped and stared at desk sergeant Charlie Middleton. Charlie would have eaten his constables alive if they had taken a private call and it was unusual for Charlie to listen so intently to anybody. When Charlie put the phone down, he looked at the detective.

"Hunter, I need your help. My sister's assistant in her sandwich shop, Abbie MacLeod, has had her wee one stolen. We need to get her back."

"That's your sister Laura, right?"

"Aye."

"Call upstairs to get whoever is there to join me in the incident room. You can give us the details now and we'll start work right away."

"Thanks Hunter. You're not always the bastard I paint you."

"Thanks, I think!"

The team gathered in the incident room. DCs Tim Myerscough and Bear Zewedu stood at the back and took up more space than two humans usually would. DS Colin Read sat eating an apple beside DC Nadia Chan who was halfway through a luke-warm mug of tea and DC Mel Grant wandered in carrying three mugs of coffee for Tim, Bear, and herself.

"I heard this is about Abbie MacLeod, boss," Mel said. She handed out the coffees and offered KitKats to Tim and Bear from her trouser pocket. "Isn't that the girl we got for killing an old woman three or four years back? And now she's lost her baby? I mean, really! The kid's probably better off with whoever took her, doesn't matter who it is."

"I doubt it, DC Grant." Sergeant Charlie Middleton replied. "The child was taken by her father, Josh Bryden."

"Oh God!" Mel sighed. "That kid's got no chance. Bryden is really bad news. How does he stay out of our grasp?"

"He's clever and he gets others to take the fall for him," Hunter said. "Charlie, can you explain to the team what happened this morning?"

When Charlie Middleton came to the end of his briefing, he turned to Hunter. "Abbie's grandmother, Barbara MacLeod, has full legal custody of the child, boss. She's been a friend of Laura's since God was a boy."

"That's a name I don't know," Hunter said.

"No boss, Barbara's real salt of the earth. She's looked after Abbie and her brother, Lewis, since their parents died in a traffic accident ten years ago."

"So how come Abbie got into so much trouble?" Mel asked.

"She fell under the spell of Josh Bryden, and he left her to carry the can, so I'm told."

"Silly bitch." Mel muttered.

"Silly, possible, young and impressionable probably," Hunter said.

"I honestly believe Abbie is trying to make a go of things and get it right now. Laura does too, that's why she gave her a job. Hunter, if it's all right with you, I'm going to get myself over to Laura's shop to take statements and see the lie of the land."

"Yes of course, Charlie. Keep me posted."

"Do we want this in the public domain?" Colin asked.

"No, not yet" Hunter said. "If this becomes public knowledge, Abbie's past will come out and opinion will mirror Mel's and that's not relevant. We must find the child and return her to her legal guardian - not either of her parents."

Colin nodded. "I agree. And everyone is entitled to a second chance."

"Colin, I want you and Nadia to go through all we have on Josh Bryden and his accomplices."

Tim looked up from his phone. "It's amazing what people put on social media – Josh has just put up a picture of him with his wee girl on Facebook. It says they're at the shopping centre in Wester Hailes."

"There's one on Instagram too." Bear muttered.

"Good he's got his phone on, get the boffins to trace that."

Bear left the room and strode along the corridor to the computer experts who would find the information.

"I've got an address, boss. And it's in Wester Hailes." Nadia handed the information to Hunter.

"That was quick!"

"Not really," Nadia said. "I got it off his charge sheet from when we brought him in for possession last year. Looks like we just gave him a caution."

"Hmm. Okay, you and Colin keep digging. Get Bear to keep the pressure on the boffins. I want that phone number and an exact location."

"Will do, boss."

"Mel, I need you to do a full background check on Abbie. I need to know that the child will be safe if they're both living with her grandmother."

"Yes. Will do."

"Tim, you're with me."

"My car or a pool car?"

"Don't ask stupid questions, young Myerscough."

Tim led the way down the stairs and unlocked his large, comfortable hybrid BMW. He slipped into the driver's seat and waited for Hunter to follow him down the stairs.

"You know, boss, I'm just wondering how Josh knew where Abbie worked and where the kid was. Did Abbie tell him? How else would he know where to look for her?"

"Good questions but I don't know the answers."

. . .

Hunter led Tim into the block of flats that Nadia had advised them Josh lived in. "Thirteenth floor, why doesn't that surprise me?"

Tim pressed the button to call the lift. Nothing happened.

"Fuck!" Hunter turned towards the stairs.

"Boss, I'll run up and check it out."

"Run?"

"Yes, it can be my training for today."

"What if there's trouble? I better come."

Tim pulled himself up to his full height and puffed out his chest.

"Aye, I know you're a big guy, but what if he's got a knife?"

"Then by the time I'm finished, I'll have a knife." Tim smiled. "Look boss, I don't think he's there, the photos were from the shopping centre, but you wanted to rule out his flat first. Even if he is at home, I'll cope."

Hunter shook his head. "Fine. I'll call Charlie and learn what he's got from Laura. But shout if you need me."

Tim took the stairs two at a time and wasn't breathless when he got to the thirteenth floor. A youngster was standing guard outside one of the flats.

"You should be at school," Tim said.

"And you should mind your own business."

"Looking for Josh Bryden. Do you know him?"

"What if I do?"

Hunter arrived on the landing. He flipped open his identification.

"Police looking to speak to him."

Tim smiled. "Hi boss," he said. "Young Lewis here is a friend of Josh's."

"How'd you know my name, big man?"

"It's all that made sense. Somebody had to be stupid and gullible enough to be talked into joining Josh and tell him about Abbie. And it had to be someone Abbie trusted."

The kid lunged at Tim with a sharp kitchen knife.

"Who you calling stupid?"

Tim caught the boy's arm and squeezed his hand until he dropped the knife. Then he flicked him over into a half nelson and laid him on the floor. Now Lewis was sprawled across the landing, Tim held him there and asked Hunter to cuff the lad.

"What else have you got in those pockets?" Hunter growled.

"Nothing!"

"Search him, DC Myerscough."

Tim searched Lewis and found a set of keys. "These the keys to this place?" He nodded at the door of the flat.

Just at that point they heard a squeal come from inside the property.

"What the hell was that?" Hunter looked at Tim.

The door opened.

Hunter and Josh Bryden recognised each other instantly. Josh was nursing his hand. He made to slam the door, but Tim was holding it open with his foot.

"What happened to your hand, Josh? It has little bite marks on it. Perhaps I can help?" Hunter asked.

"Fuck off Sergeant Wilson, it's nothing. And what the hell is he doing on the floor outside my flat?"

"It's DI Wilson to you, now."

"Lah-di-dah."

"And young Lewis here was just about to tell us where your daughter is."

"He fuckin' wasn't and anyway, I've never seen this lad before." Josh kicked Lewis's leg. It was the only part of him he could reach without leaving his door unguarded.

Hunter smiled. "That's assault, Josh. I'll have to arrest you for that."

"Boss, while you do that, is it necessary for me to search the flat? After all, if it wasn't Josh who was injured we must have heard somebody else cry out. There could be a threat to life."

"A threat to life? Aye your life, copper, if you try to come into my place."

"Threatening my colleague, now?" Hunter asked.

Tim smiled with his head on one side. "Come ahead if you really fancy your chances."

"Josh, we'll have to insist on coming in to ensure nobody is seriously injured," Hunter said. "You can let us in voluntarily or not, your choice."

Josh was still nursing his hand when he opened the door wider and waved Tim inside. "Just you. Take a look." Then he turned to Lewis, "You're fuckin' dead, you numpty."

Hunter stood toe to toe with Josh at the door. Lewis was still strewn across the floor while the three of them waited for Tim to return. Five minutes later, he came back to the entrance.

"I can't see anybody, boss. There's certainly no sign of Daisy."

Josh grinned. "Now will you leave my bloody home alone and take that scab of humanity with you? It'll save me having to sort him out." He growled at Lewis.

Then they heard the unmistakable voice of a small child.

"Can I come out now, Daddy? I not in trouble for the bite? You okay? Am I the winner?"

"Hide and seek, Josh? Clever," Hunter said. "Yes, you're the winner Daisy. You're not in any trouble."

The sound of a child's footsteps ran towards them. Tim bent down and picked up the little girl. "Hello, Daisy," he said. "My name's Tim. You are incredibly good at hiding." He smiled as she nodded at him. "Can you show me your best place to hide and win the game?" He put her back down and she held his hand, leading the way into the living room.

She crawled down the side of the biggest leather couch by the bookcase and wiggled behind it.

"I win here!" She called out.

"Gosh, you should be careful you don't get hurt behind there." Tim pulled the sofa forwards and noticed a loose floorboard behind it. "See this could scratch you." He tugged at the board until it came free.

Josh heard the noise and ran from the door. "Get away! You got no warrant." He shouted.

Tim looked at the jewellery, watches and cash hidden under the floor. "And you got no right to let your daughter hide where she might get hurt and, I guess, no right to the things hidden here."

Hunter smiled at Tim as he led the little girl back towards the door of the flat. "Let's get Daisy returned to her legal guardian, Barbara McLeod, and you can argue the toss about the lack of a warrant back at the station. After all, you invited Tim in, and I stayed right here."

Hunter heard the door of the close open and heard people running up the stairs. "Oh Lord, what now?" He muttered.

"Oh, boss you're here," Mel said.

"It's those powers of observation that made you the detective you are today, DC Grant."

"It's just that the boffins found Josh had moved from the shopping centre to here and we couldn't get hold of you or Tim, so we came to look for Daisy," Bear said.

Hunter tapped his pockets. "My bloody phone's on silent! Where's yours Tim?"

"Must have left it in the car."

Hunter shook his head and took the opportunity to phone Charlie Middleton to give him the good news that they had found Daisy and Josh was being brought in for questioning.

"If you take Barbara MacLeod home, Charlie; Tim and I will bring the wee one round. Send a couple of Uniforms to pick up Josh will you?... No, he won't be going anywhere, Mel and Bear are here and will wait for your boys.... No they can't bring him in, they'll be bringing Lewis MacLeod to the station.... The charge against Lewis? We'll start with attempted assault with a deadly weapon and work from there."

ACKNOWLEDGMENTS

Writing is often portrayed as a lonely occupation but while the stories created here are the products of one mind, the process as a whole is far from solitary.

First, I want to thank my beta readers and those who took time to read an early draft, critique and endorse *Hunter's Christmas and Other Stories*. Particular mentions go to Anna MacDonald, Chris Maughan and Libbie Fisher for their encouragement and help in offering suggestions.

I am also grateful to my editors, Steph Patterson, and Nikki East who are amongst the most patient people I have ever met. A good editor tears apart a story and makes it better.

I thank all at SpellBound Books, including Sumaira Wilson and Nikki East for their encouragement and inspiration throughout my work on *Hunter's Christmas and Other Stories.* Without them, this book would not exist. I am also grateful to those who gave me medical and technical advice. Of course, any mistakes are mine.

My long-suffering and supportive husband, Dave deserves a special mention for his unconditional support as do our beloved girls, Lizzie, Vicky, and Becca. And to each one of my readers, thank you very much. I am thrilled you continue to enjoy my stories.

ABOUT THE AUTHOR

Val Penny has an Llb degree from the University of Edinburgh and her MSc from Napier University. She has had many jobs including hairdresser, waitress, banker, azalea farmer and lecturer but has not yet achieved either of her childhood dreams of being a ballerina or owning a candy store.

Until those dreams come true, she has turned her hand to writing poetry, short stories, nonfiction books, and novels. Her novels are published by SpellBound Books Ltd.

Val is an American author living in SW Scotland. She has two adult daughters of whom she is justly proud and the most adorable granddaughter. She lives with her husband and their cat.

Printed in Great Britain
by Amazon

35601842R00117